DIDN'T STAY IN VEGAS

CHELSEA M. CAMERON

Get Free Books!

Tropetastic romance with a twist, Happily Ever Afters guaranteed! You can expect humor and heart in every Chelsea M. Cameron romance.

Get a free book today! Join Chelsea's Newsletter and get a copy of Marriage of Unconvenience, about two best friends who get fake married to share an inheritance and end up with a lot of *real* feelings.

And now, back to Didn't Stay in Vegas…

About Didn't Stay in Vegas

Sometimes what happens in Vegas doesn't stay there.

Callyn Stott wakes up from a night-out at her friend Lara's Bachelorette party in Vegas with a hangover… and a wife. She's not really sure how she and her best friend Emma got hitched, only that they did and it's completely and totally legal. Callyn is used to getting in and out of scrapes, but this one takes the cake.

Further complicating matters, Emma suggest that they stay married for "financial reasons" that don't really hold water. Not wanting to argue, Callyn agrees. The situation gets even more confusing when Callyn has to move out of her apartment, and where is she going to stay? With her fake wife, and best friend, of course. It's not like anything is going to happen. Things between the two of them have always been strictly platonic and best-friendy, right? Emma hasn't been secretly in love with Callyn her whole life and has just been waiting for Callyn to notice. No, surely not.

Will Callyn get her head out of her ass and see what's right in front of her, or will she live the rest of her life oblivious that the one person she's always wanted is already there?

Chapter One

I woke up with glitter in my junk. Granted, I also woke up wearing a dress I didn't remember buying, in a bed I'd never seen before, and with the worst hangover in the history of time. I had to pee as if I'd drunk twelve gallons of liquid and, judging by the intensity of the hangover pounding in my body, I might have had that much in alcoholic beverages.

I groped my way around the too-bright room and found the bathroom, shielding my eyes from the pure white marble and gaudy gold accents. I yanked up the dress to find (with relief) that I was wearing underwear, but then a shower of glitter fell to the white marble floor.

"The fuck?" I said, taking my underwear fully down and folding myself in half to glare at my junk. What was going on down there?

Glitter. Glitter all up in there. Why in the hell did I have glitter on my vulva? I peed and attempted to wipe the glitter off with toilet paper, but it was a lost cause.

Giving up on that, I decided to crawl to the shower and wash when I heard a moan. I guess wasn't alone in the strange, ostentatious hotel room. I grabbed the closest gold vase and raised it up, preparing to defend myself as I peered around the doorway. Sprawled on a purple velvet couch across from the bed was—

"Emma," I breathed out, lowering the vase and putting it back on the counter. She let out another moan and then opened her eyes, raising her head slowly and blinking a few times.

"The fuck?" she said, struggling to get into a sitting position. She also wore a sequin-drenched gown that was cut down to her navel in the front. Holy mother of cleavage. One of her boobs was making a break for freedom, so I tried to focus on her face instead. Friends didn't stare at their friend's escaping boobs, at least not on purpose.

"I don't know," I said. "But I just peed glitter." Emma squinted her green eyes at me and started to laugh, but then groaned and put both hands on her head, her fingers tangling in her dark hair. "That was a bad idea."

My brain had started to sharpen and remember where we were and why we were here.

"Vegas. We're in Vegas."

"No shit," Emma said, wiping mascara streaks down her face.

"Right, we're in Vegas for Lara's bachelorette party. But why are we *here*? This isn't the hotel we were staying at. And I do not remember putting this dress on. Or putting glitter on my downstairs," I said.

Emma finally stood up and she looked like a baby giraffe on new legs. Wobbly and uncertain.

"Now *I* have to pee, out of the way." I moved aside and she headed into the bathroom, not even bothering to shut the door. I turned my back and ignored her while she let out sounds of relief as she used the facilities and then washed her hands.

"Fucking hell," she said, putting a hand on my shoulder,

which caused me to jump. "Let's just order some room service. I need to eat or else I'm going to hurl."

"Don't say the word 'hurl,'" I said, putting my hand on my stomach. It had started rolling a few minutes before and I wanted to make sure it didn't try to turn itself inside out.

Emma found her way to the hotel phone and pulled out a menu. Flopping down on the bed and holding it in the air, she looked over at me. Her boobs were seriously about to jump out of that dress. I looked at her face.

"What do you want?" I walked slowly to the bed and sat down next to her. She smelled like the cheap perfume they'd have in a vending machine at a bar, not like her. Not like Emma.

"I don't know," I said. The words on the menu spun when I tried to read them.

"It's fine, I know your hangover order," she said, and dialed the number for room service.

"Hi, yes, we need three of the fried egg and bacon sandwiches, French fries, two biscuits, and two green smoothies . . . Yes . . . Thank you." I had to fight another round of nausea at the mention of all that food. Hopefully that would change when said food got here.

"I have to get this dress off, Callyn. Be a doll and help me." Emma turned her back to me, presenting me with the zipper in the back of the dress. My fingers trembled as I tried to grip it and pull it down at the same time.

"Sorry," I said, my hands slipping on the tiny zipper. I regained my grip and got the zipper down to her waist. Emma pushed the straps off her shoulders and sighed in relief. As far as I could tell, she wasn't wearing anything under it.

"That's so much better." She stood up and shimmied the dress down her hips, leaving it in a sequin puddle on the floor. I couldn't look as she crossed the room and pulled a thick robe from the back of the bathroom door. Yup, she had been completely naked under the dress. Sure, I'd seen her naked dozens of times before, but it was always weird and I always tried to give her privacy. The alcohol must have lowered her inhibitions, because she wasn't normally this free with nudity. Neither of us were. Vegas was a whole other place.

Moments later, the room service arrived.

"Hello, my love," Emma said, sighing happily as she pushed the cart over to the couch. "Don't you want to take that dress off and get in one of these robes?" She rubbed the material against her cheek. Judging by the state we were currently in, we'd had one hell of a night and she still looked incredible. Sure, she might have a little bit of mascara goop on her eyes, and her hair was a complete and utter disaster, but Emma was gorgeous as hell and always would be.

I went into the bathroom and struggled to dislocate my arm to reach the zipper in the back of my dress before calling out to Emma for help.

"You dork," she said, coming up behind me and undoing the zipper with little effort. I held the gown to my chest so it didn't fall. I knew I wasn't wearing any kind of bra.

"Thanks," I said, and she handed me a robe. I put it on before sliding the dress off.

"I've seen your boobs before," Emma said. "How many years have we been friends?"

I kicked the dress aside and tied the robe securely, making sure I was covered before I turned around to face her.

"Too many," I said with a smirk, and she gasped and then hit me in the shoulder.

"Just for that I'm not giving you any of the extra bacon. It's all mine now." She rushed to the cart and snatched the plate of bacon, crouching over it like a dragon with a hoard of gold and hissed.

"My bacon," she said in a deep, demonic voice, that made the hair on the back of my next stand on end.

"Please don't use that voice. You know it freaks me out." I joined her on the couch, reaching instead for a plate with the sandwiches on it. I took a tiny bite, willing my stomach to behave itself. After a few small bites, I was a little more confident that I could keep the food down.

Emma was going to town on the bacon and at last held out one strip to me, like it was a fresh-picked rose.

"Callyn, will you accept this bacon?" she said, using a phrase from a popular reality dating show.

"Yes, I will," I said, completely serious, reaching out to take the bacon and then shoved it in my mouth. It was just the right amount of crispy and chewy. Shit, I loved room service.

Emma moved on to the sandwiches and I figured I needed something green, so I sucked down a smoothie. A beep startled both of us and we went on a quest to find the source of it only to hear additional beeping across the room. Both of our phones were blowing up.

We'd been so wrapped up in dealing with hangovers and getting food into us that we hadn't gotten to how the hell we'd made it into this room last night (or this morning), how we'd gotten the gowns, and what had happened to lead up to all of that. I'd tried to think, but my brain screamed in protest every time.

"Oh, crap."

"What's up?" I said, tearing through the covers on the bed and sending my phone flying to the floor. I dove for it before it could bounce off the carpet and go under the bed. My clumsy thumbs scrolled through my missed messages.

Oh. Oh *shit*. Most of them were my friends asking where

Emma and I were, and they got increasingly more panicked the later it had gotten. Luckily, we were all in a group text together, so I could respond to everyone at once. Just a second before I hit Send, the reply from Emma popped up.

We're both fine. In a hotel somewhere, will figure everything out and meet you there soon.

I sent my message agreeing with her and a flood of relieved replies came in asking for all the dirty details.

"I don't remember the details and I'm pretty sure they weren't dirty," I said, as Emma went back to the room service cart and devoured more of the food. "Well, except for the glitter. Do you have any idea why I would have had glitter on my downstairs?" I blushed when I said that for some reason. I'd always been weird about that stuff with her. She might be my best friend, but there were lines I just didn't cross with Emma.

"I think there was something about a kit where you could jazz it up down there and someone dared you to do it, maybe?" Right. A dare. I was a sucker for dares, which had gotten me into much worse trouble than having glitter on my vulva before.

"Why didn't you stop me?" I had zero recollection of this event.

Emma gave me a look.

"Have I ever been able to stop you when you put your mind to something?" I opened my mouth to argue, but then snapped it shut.

"Fair enough," I said with a sigh, flopping down on the couch. The group chat was racing again, and I decided we needed to figure out where the hell we were and how to get back to our friends. I found the notepad with the hotel name and address on it and put it into my phone to figure out how far away we were from our friends' hotel.

"We're only a ten-minute walk down the strip," I said.

"How did we even end up here? You seem to have a better memory than me." That was entirely unfair. I hoped as the day wore on the hangover wore off that my memory would get clearer.

"Can we take a cab? I don't want to walk. Or maybe we could have someone come and bring us some clothes? I'm not super into the idea of a walk of shame with that getup on." Yeah, I wasn't into that idea either. I sent a quick message asking if anyone could meet us with some regular clothes. Nova said she would and I thanked her profusely.

Emma and I finished most of the food and then there was a knock at the door. I rushed to open it, finding Nova grinning on the other side with a bag slung over her arm.

"You two are ridiculous," she said, breezing in as if she didn't have a hint of a hangover at all. Her dark brown skin glowed, and I knew that she wasn't even wearing any makeup. Having a friend so pretty was painful sometimes.

"Yes, but in the best way," Emma said, reaching for the bag and then heading to the bathroom to change.

"So, what have you two been doing all night?" Nova said after Emma shut the door. Was it my imagination that she said it in a suggestive way? Weird.

"Honestly, I don't know. But I was wearing a sequined dress and somehow we got here." I gestured around the room.

"I'm sure it's going to be a great story when you remember it," Nova said. Emma came out of the bathroom in a simple white tank and jeans with holes in the knees.

"So much better," she said, sitting on the couch.

"My turn," I said, grabbing the bag from her. I dashed to the bathroom and shut the door. I wanted to change, but also to wipe off some more of the glitter if I could. There were some makeup wipes on the counter and I scrubbed as good as I could before slipping on a new pair of undies, jeans, and a tank with a chubby octopus on it. I combed my fingers through my hair, getting my hands stuck on a whole lot of hairspray. I needed a shower more than I needed anything else right now.

Just as I walked back out, there was another knock at the door.

"Who could that be?" Emma asked. Nova shrugged.

"Maybe housekeeping? We should get out of here anyway. I hope it's not going to cost me too much." I wasn't exactly rolling in money right now. This trip had been a splurge already.

Nova went and looked out the peephole.

"Looks like room service or something?" I shared a glance with Emma.

"No idea, since we already ate and put the cart out. I guess open up and see? They probably have the wrong room," I said. Nova opened the door and had a quick chat with the person outside and then turned around slowly, the door still open.

"Um, so, this is Craig and he's here to bring a complimentary honeymoon breakfast to the newlyweds." She said all this with her brown eyes so wide I thought they were going to fall out of her head.

"The what to the who?" I asked, and Emma burst out laughing.

"We must have told them we got married to get free stuff," Emma whispered at me as Craig wheeled the cart in. This one was draped in gaudy red velvet and included an ice bucket with champagne, chocolate strawberries, and two dishes covered in silver. Oh, and two red roses. Cute.

"Thank you so much, Craig," Nova said, pulling some cash out of her bag and handing it to him.

"Congratulations," Craig said, giving us a grin before he departed.

"What *did* you get up to last night?" Nova said, snatching a strawberry off the tray.

"Still hazy," I said, joining her and going for a strawberry for myself.

"Let's enjoy this and then head back. I'm ready to end this weekend right," Emma said. She got up and stopped.

"What's that?" she said. I looked down and saw a sheet of paper shoved halfway under the couch. Emma bent down and picked it up. Then her eyes went as wide as Nova's had been when she'd opened the door.

"What is it?" I asked, setting down a third strawberry. Emma's face had gone paler than I'd ever seen it before, so something on that paper had given her a shock. Her hand shook as she held it out to me without a word. I only needed to read the top scrolling words and see the seal, as well as our signatures to realize why she was flipping out.

"You two look like someone died, what the hell?" Nova asked, abandoning the cart.

"Nope. No one's dead. We're just a little bit married."

Chapter Two

"You're fucking kidding me," Nova said, as Emma and I stared at the certificate of our marriage. My signature was a little messy, but it was definitely mine. We also found a little bag of gifts from the wedding chapel we'd gone to (which was right behind the hotel), including two cheap rings that looked as if they'd been pulled out of a vending machine.

"Maybe it's a joke certificate?" Nova questioned. "I mean, I'm sure they print those, right?"

"Looks pretty real to me," I said.

"Yup, it's real all right," Emma said, holding her phone up. She had the website of the chapel up on her phone and there we were, holding each other like we were at a high school prom and laughing our asses off.

"I mean, you're impulsive, but this is next level, Callyn, Jesus," Emma said, pacing the living room area, one hand tangling through her hair.

"Um, excuse me? Why is this my fault? I don't remember what the fuck happened, how do you know it was my idea?" I threw my hands up and sat on the couch. How had this happened? Why couldn't I remember anything? This couldn't have been my idea. Most of my impulses were to do things like order pizza at three in the morning, or go drive up a mountain and watch the sun rise. Not marriage. Nothing like that.

"Well, it wasn't *my* idea," Emma said, pivoting to face me.

"It was *someone's* idea, because you've got this shiny certificate here," Nova said, waving the paper in the air. She had a look on her face as if she wanted to laugh, but was holding back. Right now, this didn't seem all that funny. Maybe in a few hours it would. Right now, all I could feel was shock and panic.

"Look, it's no big deal, I'm sure this happens all the time. You can just get it annulled," Nova said. "I'm sure it's a simple process. Come on, let's go end this weekend right." I looked at Emma and sighed. There was nothing to be done about it now. Nova rolled up the certificate and handed it to me.

"Fine," Emma said, getting up. "I guess we'll figure it out later."

"I thought I was going to go home with a sunburn and maybe some extra cash from the casinos. But no, I'm coming home with a wife." Emma gave me a look.

"What, too soon?" I said, bopping her on the head with our marriage certificate.

∾

I THOUGHT about not telling our friends about the whole marriage fiasco, but that didn't last when we walked back into the suite we'd been staying in.

"So, we got married," I said, unfurling the certificate. Emma sighed beside me. They'd been lounging around in the common area, drinking mimosas, but at my announcement, they all stood up and rushed over.

"You did what now?" Lara, the bride-to-be asked.

"I thought we weren't going to talk about it yet, but yes, we apparently left you all last night and got married," Emma said, glaring at me for a moment.

"We didn't agree *not* to talk about it. I mean, I couldn't keep something like this to myself and you know that." I could definitely keep my mouth shut when it came to protecting people, or telling white lies, but this wasn't the kind of thing I could hold in for long. Plus, Nova probably would have said something to her girlfriend Sammi, and then Sammi would have told. Sammi wasn't the best one with secrets, that was for sure, bless her.

"You got *married*?" Willa cried, putting down her glass and reaching for the certificate. "Like, married, *married*? With vows and everything?" I looked at Emma and then shrugged.

"I guess? I mean, I don't remember anything beyond going to the bar after the magic show." I reached and searched within my mind, but everything got hazy. I'd had a lot to drink. Shots upon shots upon mixed drinks. I'd decided that I was going to live it up this weekend, and that had seriously backfired.

"Yeah, we had a lot of drinks. I'm hurting today for sure," Lara said, even though her brown eyes were clear and her hair was perfect.

"So what, you just get it annulled, right? I'm sure you can probably do that online," Sammi said, leaning against Nova.

"I guess," I said. "We'll deal with that later." I was suddenly very tired.

"We'll deal with it later," Emma said in a quiet voice. She wouldn't meet my eyes. She shook her head and then smiled, but it didn't seem genuine. "We still have one day and one night left, so I say we keep celebrating Lara, since that's what we're here to do." She picked up a glass and filled it with orange juice and champagne before handing it to me and then making another for herself.

"To Lara," she said, raising her glass. We all raised ours and toasted.

"To Lara!"

After consuming several mimosas, we headed to the spa in the hotel for hot stone massages, facials, and pedicures. It was the perfect way to end the weekend that had been filled with gambling, dancing, drinking, and just being fools before we had to go back to our regular lives with jobs and bills and responsibilities. It was also a hell of a detox.

"Hey," Emma said, as we got our pedicures. She'd been pretty damn quiet the whole day. Emma was my best friend and, for the first time ever, I was at a loss for what to say.

"Hey," I said, leaning closer to her as the nail tech scrubbed the bottoms of my feet. It tickled just enough to be distracting.

"Are you okay?" she asked. "About this whole marriage thing?" I shrugged one shoulder. Bits and pieces had started to come back to me. I couldn't remember how we'd gotten separated from the group, but I did recall us stumbling into a shop and buying the gowns. At least I had that, and I had one more thing: the swelling feeling of joy as I looked into her eyes and said the vows the justice performing the ceremony told me to repeat. That feeling had crept back and now I couldn't stop thinking about it.

"Yeah, why?" I asked, my voice a little choked. I was going to blame it on the tech going to town on my heels.

"Just checking. I mean, I still can't remember how it happened, but it will be okay, right? We should probably not tell anyone else about it though." I agreed on that. I could just picture the particular way a frown would flip my mother's normally smiling mouth upside down, and the exact tone of the sigh my father would let out. *Reckless Callyn, at it again. Foolish Callyn. Always getting herself into one situation or another.* To be fair, I could (usually) get myself out of the scrapes I go into without too much damage. Most of the time.

"Yeah, I don't think my parents would be excited about this one. And I'm definitely not telling Dani," I said. Perfect Dani, my older sister who was the prettiest, smartest, most perfect daughter to ever live, according to my parents. No, I wasn't bitter about it at *all*.

"No, I'm not telling mine either. They're not so happy with me right now about the whole job-quitting thing." Emma had left her job in finance to go back to school and get her vet tech degree. It was something she'd always wanted to do, but had caved to parental pressure about making money for years.

Well, she'd made decent money, but she was so miserable that something had to give. I was so fucking proud of her for standing her ground and doing what she wanted. Since she was an only child, her parent's expectations had sat atop her shoulders and nearly crushed her spirit for most of her life.

"Let them be mad. It's not their life." She sighed and rested her head back on the massage chair, closing her eyes.

"I know that they want me secure financially because they never were. But I think I can make a little less money and be a lot happier, and they can't seem to get that." No, they never would. My parents were just happy that I had a full-time job and was living (with roommates) on my own.

"They'll see. When you graduate and start working, they'll see." I hoped they would. I hoped they could put aside their own desires and support their only daughter.

"I looked up annulments. We can file everything online. It might cost a little bit, but I'll take care of it," she said. I cringed because Emma took care of a lot of things when it came to money. I didn't want to feel ashamed that she used to make more than I did and had saved a ton, but I couldn't stop when she always whipped out her card to pay for lunch or the movies when we went out.

"We can split it," I said. "Or is that you admitting that the marriage was your idea?" That was what I wanted to know, even if it meant that I'd been the instigator. I usually was.

"Who was the one who convinced me to get a cherry tattoo on my ass?" she asked, leaning close so no one could overhear. I stifled a laugh.

"I got one too. And no one forced you to get it, Emma," I said. It had been a silly best friend thing we'd done before we'd graduated college. It was cute as hell and my parents still didn't know about it.

"And who was the one who almost got us arrested?"

"Which time?" I said with a grin. Emma tried to suppress a smile and failed. "My point is, when it comes to which one of us is more likely to say 'hey, let's get married in Vegas,' it's you."

"But maybe that's why it's *you*. Because you're assuming it's me and you should never assume." I wagged my finger at her and she grabbed it and bit it lightly before giving it back to me. My heart thumped at the thought of my finger in her mouth. What a weird thought.

We finished our pedicures, Emma getting a soft gray on her nails and me with a wild red with rhinestones on my big toes.

"Those are going to chip off in about five seconds," Emma said as I wiggled my toes and admired them.

"I don't care. They're fun."

We headed to lunch and then spent the rest of the afternoon in the hotel, watching shows about terrible people buying houses, ordering too much room service, and procrastinating on packing up our shit.

My mom sent me a message and I said that we were still in Vegas but coming back to Boston that night. I had to work tomorrow because I only had so many vacation days and I'd used them all for this trip. C'est la vie. I needed a new job. I'd already been looking and was hoping I would have some interviews soon. Mom would flip if she knew I was leaving my "stable" job doing customer service at a hotel for something else. She was always after me to apply for promotions, but I would rather let rabid squirrels slowly devour me alive than work another year at the hotel.

"When's our flight?" I called out, as I shoved the pile of my discarded clothes in my suitcase and then crammed the lid shut, sitting on it to get the zipper to close. I had folded and rolled everything to get it in there before the trip, but I wasn't going to do that now since I was just going to dump everything in the washer when I got back.

"Hurry up, Callyn!" was the response from everyone who was already standing at the hotel suite door with their meticulously packed suitcases. Whatever, we'd get there in time.

I rolled my suitcase out and saw everyone breathe a sigh of relief.

"Let me do one last check," I said. I'd left more than one item behind in a hotel room in my life. I rushed around the room as my friends tried not to be too annoyed. They should know me by now.

"Did you get it?" Emma asked, as I scanned the couch for any clothing item I might have strewn on it.

"Get what?" I asked, pushing the pillows aside.

"The marriage certificate? You had it last." Holy shit, I'd forgotten about that for all of ten minutes. Marriage certificate.

"Right. I think I had it in the room." I dashed into the bedroom where I'd been spending my time. It had last been on the dresser? The desk? Something like that. I didn't see anything. I tore through the room and then came out to the living room and then tried the bathroom.

"I can't find it!" I yelled after I'd checked the tub.

"Yeah, that's because I have it," Emma called back to me.

"What?" I shrieked and ran out to the main part of the suite. Emma was there, smirking and holding the marriage certificate in her hand. "Didn't want to lose it." I narrowed my eyes slowly and held my hand out for it.

"No way. I'm keeping this safe." She went to the desk in the room and found a folder in one drawer, slid the certificate inside it, and then put that in the front pocket of her suitcase.

"There. Now we won't lose it."

"I wouldn't have lost it," I said, but there was definitely a chance I might have. I lost a lot of things; it was my nature.

"I know," Emma said, her voice softening. "But you know what a control freak I am." That was Emma's nature, and I was used to it by now.

"Can we go, *please*?" Lara said, staring at her phone. "The van will be here in one minute." We all hustled ourselves to the elevator and then out to the front of the hotel.

"Holy hell," I said, instantly breaking out in a sweat. Boston could get hot, but not like this.

We all piled into the van and made our way to the airport. Thanks to Emma's meticulous planning, we were there in plenty of time to get through the security line and be at our gate and chill for a whole hour before our flight started boarding.

"I'm tired as fuck," I said, resting my head on Emma's shoulder. I planned on crashing out and sleeping the whole way home. Emma shifted beside me.

"Stay still," I whined. Her shoulder was the perfect

height for me to lean on. There were so many reasons we worked as best friends.

"Sorry, my shoulder is sore." I picked my head up and looked at her.

"Did you hurt it? Do you want me to rub it for you?" I wiggled my fingers. One of my many talents was a damn good deep tissue massage. If I didn't hate making small talk and seeing random strangers naked, I might have gone into massage therapy.

"No, it's fine," she said, leaning away from me. She was being weird again, and it worried me. Emma didn't hide things from me, ever. Emma knew the deepest darkest corners of my soul, and I knew hers.

"You okay?" I asked, hoping she would cave and tell me that she'd started her period early (we were on the same cycle and I wasn't due for another few days), or that she was having stomach cramps from the airport sushi she insisted on buying earlier. Something told me it was neither of those things.

"Yeah, just tired," she said. "Thinking about a lot."

"You mean the fact that we got married and now we have to sort that out?" I asked. She winced just a little when I mentioned the getting married.

"No, I'd completely forgotten about that," she said in a deadpan voice.

"This is one thing that isn't going to stay in Vegas," I said with a sigh. I hoped it wouldn't be too hard to sort out. I hadn't looked up what it would require to annul the thing because I was scared of the cost, and the amount of hoops we'd have to jump through. There was a girl at work who was in law school, so my plan was to ask her to look it up and explain the legal jargon to me so I could understand it. And that was if Emma didn't figure it out before me. I had the feeling she would. Emma was always on top of things, unlike me. I wanted to show her that I could handle this, for once.

"I'm going to hear that joke a lot, aren't I?" she said, meeting my eyes. Hers were sometimes blue, sometimes green. Right now they were shading toward green with the harsh airport light.

"Yes, for the rest of our lives. You know you're stuck with me." She'd been stuck with me since the third grade when I had tackled a boy making fun of her on the first day of school. She was new in town and I couldn't take my eyes off her pretty dark hair and blue-green eyes. I hadn't even known her name yet, but that boy was a jerk to a lot of girls and I hadn't wanted him to hurt the girl with the beautiful ponytail. That was all it took for us to bond for life.

Emma knew me better than I knew myself, and vice versa. We'd been physically apart for a few years there for college (she ended up going to her parent's choice of school instead of her own), but we never lost touch. Even if we hadn't talked for weeks, we picked up right where we'd left off, as if we'd just taken a pause in the middle of one lifelong conversation.

"Forever," she whispered, so low that I could barely hear it.

∼

WE MADE it back from Vegas in one piece, but a little worse for wear. The next day at work was totally brutal. There had been a convention that weekend and we'd had a glitch with the computer system, so people had gotten charged double for their rooms. I was in tears before ten in the morning, and not just because I was exhausted.

"Do you need to take ten and cry in the bathroom?" my coworker Linda asked, with a sympathetic smile. I'd been wiping my eyes while listening to a particularly nasty woman berate me on the phone.

"Yup," I said, getting up and wiping my nose with a tissue. I kept a full box on my desk for days like this.

"I'll cover you," Linda said. She was about my mom's age and I think, now that her daughter lived in Florida, she had adopted me as a surrogate daughter.

I got done with my crying fit, splashed some water on my face, and went back to my desk. I had to get the fuck away from this place. Jessika, my law-school coworker, had called in sick, so I couldn't ask her about the annulment, which I'd been wanting to do. This Monday was doing its best to mess with me.

Somehow I made it through the rest of the day and, instead of going to my apartment and dealing with one or both of my roommates, I sent a message to Emma and said that I'd stop and grab wings, cheesy garlic bread, and sodas if she would let me hang out in her apartment for a little while. Emma lived alone, and being with her was the next best thing to being alone. There was always someone or several someones at my place and it was hard to deal with sometimes.

She agreed and said that she'd throw something in the oven for dessert. I wrote back asking what it was, but she just replied that I would find out when I got there. Emma always surprised me with sweets. It had started when we were kids and she'd have cookies or cakes or some other sweet thing in her lunchbox every day. It was my job to guess what the item was and then she'd always pull out an extra for me. She would let me guess until I got it right, even giving me hints so I wouldn't have to wait too long. It never occurred to me that she had to sneak extras for me every day because her mom wasn't the one putting in the extra desserts. Emma had always had my back, even then.

Once we'd gotten older, she'd kept up the game when I would come over for dinner, making all kinds of things from crepes with homemade jam to lemon tarts to macarons to mini cheesecakes with multiple layers that were so perfect, they could have been sold in a patisserie. She was a dessert genius, but it was a hobby that she didn't want to monetize because hey, when you took a passion and made it a job, you sucked a lot of the fun out of it. If I were talented at anything, I'd probably feel the same way.

I started sending Emma guesses immediately. I kept a running list of what she'd made me before since she didn't make the same thing twice within a short time span.

Emma buzzed me into the apartment and the scent of warm chocolate hit me in the face as I opened her door. I never bothered to knock when I came over.

"Brownies?" I yelled out.

"Nope," she called from the kitchen. If Emma ever made anything as common as brownies, they'd be baked with expensive chocolate and layered with marzipan or something. I didn't even know what marzipan was, but it sounded like something that rich people would eat.

"Chocolate," I said to myself, scanning my list. "Hmm." I set the bag of wings, garlic bread, and sodas on the counter as she peered into the oven. I tried to see over her shoulder, but she quickly moved and blocked my view before slamming the oven door and spinning around to face me, using her body as a shield between me and the baking dessert.

"I don't think so. You don't get it until you guess right." I huffed before grabbing a stool and sitting at the little kitchen island that was just big enough for two.

I decided to do what any self-respecting woman with a smartphone would do: I looked up and named every single kind of chocolate dessert I could find.

"Nope," Emma said, digging into the bag of food and

yanking out the box of wings. If I didn't hurry up and guess the dessert right then, I was going to lose out on the wings.

"Mousse? Cupcakes? Chocolate Cream pie?"

"No, no, no," she said, sucking sauce off her fingers. My brain blanked for a second and I couldn't remember what I was supposed to be doing.

"You going to keep guessing?" Emma asked, discarding the bone in a bowl. I snatched a wing out of the box, eating it with one hand and scrolling my phone with the other.

Eventually, I gave up and let Emma wear the smug smile of victory because I was hungry and I knew she was going to give me whatever it was anyway. Emma broke the garlic bread in half, putting some on a plate and pushing it toward me.

"Hey, you gave me the smaller half," I said, checking it against the half she'd taken for herself.

"You got an extra wing. The number was uneven."

"Oh," I said. "That's okay then." I devoured the bread and Emma asked me if I wanted some wine. She had a new bottle of a sweet and spicy red that she thought I might like.

"Just one glass," I said. "I'm still suffering from this weekend. Why did we decide to go to Vegas? All of that stuff wouldn't have happened if we'd gone to… to… Nebraska." Emma snorted as she poured a decent-sized glass of wine for me.

"What's in Nebraska?" I took a cautious sip and my eyes rolled back in my head. Oh yeah, that was damn good. I'd have to pace myself so I didn't suck down the whole bottle in one sitting.

"I have no idea. It was the first random state to come to my mind. Anyway, whose idea was Vegas again?" Emma gave me a sardonic look.

"Yours, Callyn."

"Right," I said, pointing at her with my glass. I set it

down so I wasn't tempted to down the entire thing in one go. "Most ideas that blow up in my face are mine." I hated facing the consequences of my own actions.

"But we all agreed to it, so it wasn't completely on you."

"That's right," I said.

The timer dinged and Emma went to the oven. It was time for the big reveal. She pulled out a Bundt pan with a chocolate cake in it and then set it down to cool before getting out some more ingredients for what I assumed was frosting.

"Em, that's just a chocolate cake. I guessed that." Emma put some sugar into a mixing bowl.

"No, you didn't guess exactly what kind of cake this is. That's the rule. This is a triple-chocolate buttermilk pound cake that I'm going to glaze in chocolate and buttermilk." I grabbed the remains of the takeout bags and the bowl full of discarded bones and put them in the trash.

"Like I was going to guess that exact kind of cake? Come on, Emma. That's just mean. There's probably billions of desserts out there," I said. She smiled and turned on the mixer, making sure that the sugar didn't go flying all over the kitchen as she did it.

I watched in rapt attention as Emma made two different glazes, turned the cake out, and waited for it to cool. That was the worst part: waiting for the dessert to be ready. The apartment was too quiet so I went and turned on some music and bopped around the living room.

"Typical. Me, working my ass off to make you a cake, and you, dancing your ass off in my living room." I spun around and did a goofy little wiggle that made her laugh every single time I did it.

"One of us has to have these sweet moves," I said, doing a shimmy that I knew looked completely ridiculous. I could actually dance well, but I preferred to dance like a dork to make Emma laugh.

"You should have left those moves in Vegas," she said, but she grabbed her wine and came to join me in the living room. Her place was miles above mine in quality, since my apartment hadn't been upgraded since before I was born and hers had new everything. It was no wonder that I loved being here more than I liked being at my cramped place with the inconsistent heating and the angry dishwasher that only worked half the time and the annoying roommates.

Emma sat on the couch and I wiggled over to join her.

"How much longer until we have cake?" I whined.

"Soon. You're always so impatient." She said it with fondness, though. I knew she loved me. We wouldn't have been best friends this long if she didn't.

"Ugh, I don't want later cake. I want *now* cake." I rubbed my stomach. "I need the cake, Em. Deep in my soul." With a sigh, she got up and checked the cake.

"Still not cool yet." So she poured another glass of wine for me instead. Almost as good, I guess.

I had to wait another ten minutes for the cake to be done, for Emma to put the glaze on, and for her to take enough pictures of it for her social to be satisfied that the cake had been documented. It felt like an eternity.

"Finally," I said, picking it up in my hand and shoving one third of the piece in my mouth. Emma gasped in shock, but I just grinned at her with my cheeks full of the incredible cake.

"You cretin," she said after a moment, her lips fighting a smile. I almost choked as I chewed and swallowed the enormous piece. Maybe this had been a mistake.

I was more conservative with my second bite and I opted to use the fork instead, after slapping the piece down on a plate. Like a fucking lady.

"This is incredible. I know I inhaled it, so you think I couldn't tell, but seriously. So good. You gonna give me some to smuggle home?" I always had to hide my sweets in my room or else my roommates would eat them before you could say cupcake.

"Sure thing," she said, eating her cake in dainty bites. She was quiet tonight and I wondered if she was still thinking about this whole marrying in Vegas thing.

"What's up, wife?" I asked and her eyes snapped up from her plate.

"That's not funny."

I started licking off my fingers and she passed me a napkin. "Why not? It's not like we really meant to do it. We just got drunk." Why was she being so weird about this? "Are you worried about your parents finding out?"

She looked at her plate again and nodded slowly.

"Maybe. I just don't want them to say anything about me making bad decisions, because of quitting my job and all that." I swigged my wine.

"Shit happens. Have you looked up how difficult it would be for us to undo it yet?" I knew she had. Emma set her plate down and went to the second bedroom where she had a little office and came back with a stack of printed papers.

"Wow, okay," I said. "So you did look it up."

"One of us has to file an initial complaint. That's this." She handed me part of the stack. Ugh, it looked complicated. "I'll fill that out and get it notarized and that's the first step. It's almost $300, but I'll cover it." I winced. That was a lot of money.

"No, I'll chip in half. We should share it," I said. She sighed and took the papers back from me. I'd gotten chocolate on them. Of course.

"I'll print new ones," she said in a quiet voice. I pulled up my phone and sent her $150 for my half. Her phone made a noise that she'd gotten the payment.

"Cal, you didn't have to do that." She hardly ever called me Cal. I always liked it when she did.

"Yes, I did. And don't you dare try to send it back because I'll just keep sending it to you." She made a frustrated noise and I laughed and tucked some of her hair behind her ears. It was always perfect and shiny, as if she had a stylist with her at all times.

"I've had chocolate and now I need cuddles," I said, holding my arms out. Emma and I had always been affectionate and physically close since we were kids. I'd hugged her more than my own parents.

Emma hesitated for a second, but then I pouted and she gave in.

"Mine, mine, mine," I said, squeezing her until she made a little yelping noise.

"Can't breathe," she said, and I reluctantly loosened my stranglehold on her. I inhaled the scent of her hair and it made my heart do a little flutter. For as long as I could remember, Emma had put orange essential oil in her shampoo and conditioner. It was as much a part of her in my mind as the indefinable smell of her skin. Pure comfort.

Emma pulled away from the cuddle too soon and I sighed, but let her go. She pulled her feet up on the couch and leaned next to me, which was almost as good as snuggling.

"You ready?" she asked, grabbing the remote. There was a new episode of our favorite show out and I'd been dying to watch it, but hadn't until we could do it together.

"Yes," I said, making sure I was comfortable. I'd forgotten my fidget cube, but Emma had extras for me in the drawer of her coffee table. She handed me one. I always had to be doing something with my hands when I watched TV, and this was better than constantly cracking my knuckles or picking at my cuticles. Sometimes I crocheted or did origami, but the cube with the little buttons and rollers was ideal for something I really wanted to pay attention to.

"Do we need drinks? Do you need to pee?" she asked. I rolled my eyes at her and grabbed the remote.

"I'm fine." I hit play.

As the show wore on, I snuggled closer to Emma, eventually leaning my whole weight on her instead of the arm of the couch. She didn't seem to notice, but then I kept seeing her hands clenching and unclenching. I wanted to give her my cube, but my hands were busy with it. This show was stressful. Emma paused it when there was a lull, saying she had to pee. When she came back, I had the blanket from the back of the couch wrapped around myself like a robe.

"You gonna share?" she asked, and I lifted one corner.

"Only if you cuddle with me." I lifted the corners of the blanket like wings to envelope her.

"What is it with you and cuddles tonight?" she said, but she slid next to me and leaned into my chest with a sigh. I liked the sound of that sigh. It meant she was relaxed and content. Not going to lie, I was a little smug that Emma only made that sound when she was with me.

"I have a quota of cuddles to fill and I'm very behind. Sorry, I don't make the rules." She looked up at me, her eyelashes fluttering. Emma didn't even need mascara. I had been jealous of her lashes since we were eleven.

"You make *all* the rules, Callyn," she said. She rested her head back on my chest and I dropped the cube and put my fingers in her hair. Even better. A little moan of satisfaction escaped from her mouth as I ran my hands through the strands of her hair and massaged her scalp, especially at the base of her neck where she stored all her stress. I knew her body almost as well as my own.

"Mmmm, that feels good," she said, pressing her head into my fingers.

"See? The cuddles come with benefits for you, Em." She hit play and resumed the show and I fiddled with her hair, enjoying the silky texture of it against my fingers.

We both groaned when the episode ended on a cliffhanger (as it always did). Emma sat up and spun around to face me on the couch.

"I don't want to go back to my place. It's crowded and gross there," I said. "Don't make me go back there."

No one but me was concerned about dishes (even though we had a dishwasher?), so I always came home to a sink full of them, and overflowing trash, and dust on everything. I refused to clean more than my share because we were all adults, so the place got grungy, fast. If I wasn't so fucking broke, I would have hired a cleaning company. Maybe when I got a new job I'd do that. If I could get a better-paying job.

"You can stay if you want." Emma had a second bedroom that she used as an office slash library slash extra closet that had a small daybed for guests. I considered it my room since I was the only guest who ever stayed over. I even had clothes and everything else I could need here. Sometimes we talked about moving in together, but Emma said she liked to have her own space, and I couldn't afford the rent here, even if I was splitting it with her. Someday. Someday I wouldn't be broke as fuck.

"Thanks. I just can't deal with them tonight," I said.

We watched a movie we'd seen before and could quote effortlessly, and then I took a quick shower while she cleaned up. When I came out of the guest room after putting on my pajamas, she was standing there with two bowls of ice cream.

"You are my favorite," I said, taking the bowl from her. It was rocky road covered in rainbow sprinkles, my favorite. Emma hated it, but she kept it in the freezer for me. She was more of a mango gelato girl, so that's what she had in her bowl.

She joined me in the guest room and we sat on the bed while we ate our ice cream, trying to avoid getting brain freeze and failing. At least I failed. Emma and I used to have freeze pop eating races in the summers and I always won because I could grit my teeth through the excruciating pain, and she would give up about a third of the way through.

"Want me to brush your hair?" she asked, after we finished. I turned around and pushed my hair over my shoulder as an answer.

"Can you braid it too?" I asked. Emma could do these incredible braids and they helped my unruly hair look cute for several days without any work on my part.

"Yeah, sure." I closed my eyes as she ran the brush through my hair and then sectioned it off to start braiding. The gentle yanks of my hair were somehow soothing. I almost drifted off to sleep as she worked, humming softly to herself. I knew exactly what song she was singing.

"There you go, Callyn," she said, patting my head. My scalp was a little tight and sore, but that was fine. It was going to look great tomorrow.

"Thank you," I said, turning around and smiling at her. "You're the best."

"Yes, I am," she said, giving me a smug smile. I hit her with a pillow and she laughed. "Listen, I have to be up early tomorrow for class, so I'm going to go to bed." I made a face. "Look, not all of us are vampire insomniacs." That was true. Emma had always gone to bed earlier than I had. If only I could learn from her example and not stay up until all hours and then be exhausted the entire day.

"Fine, fine. Hugs." I always had to hug her goodnight. Tonight's hug was a little too brief for me, and then I was alone. I didn't like it.

I turned on the small TV she had in the room (mostly by my demand) and put on something mindless as I scrolled through my phone for a little while. Figuring I should at least attempt to get to sleep at a reasonable time, I pulled up my meditation app and did a quick ten minutes to try and calm my mind.

Serenity didn't last for long. I had too many thoughts. I was still determined to figure out how the marriage had happened in Vegas, but the more I tried to reach for the memories, the further away they got. Why had I gotten that drunk? I mean, I *knew* why. It was Lara's bachelorette and my job sucked and I just wanted to have a blowout with my friends. Look where that had gotten me. Married.

I sighed in frustration and pulled out my phone to scroll mindlessly until I fell asleep from pure exhaustion. It took a long, long time.

Tomorrow was going to be rough.

Chapter Three

THE REST of the week was . . . what it was. Work was hell, but I'd finally gotten a call back for a job I'd applied for at a co-working space. I liked the vibe of their website, and the job seemed like it would pay better than my current one and would hopefully lead me to cry less in the bathroom during the day.

We scheduled the interview for the following week, so I went to Emma and she drilled me on all my questions. Once I had gone through every possible question I could think of at least five times, I asked her if she'd filed for the annulment yet.

"Haven't had a chance," she said, pulling at an invisible thread on her couch. I'd been spending a lot of time here because my roommates were being insufferable. They were both in new relationships so I was hearing a lot of sex through the thin walls and I couldn't take it anymore. I didn't need to hear my roommate screaming at her girlfriend to choke her harder, thank you very much.

Emma's apartment was an oasis of quiet and peace. Plus, Emma didn't really date much so there was no worry of hearing any of that stuff. I didn't know why she didn't have a girlfriend. It didn't make any sense because she was so fucking amazing that I couldn't imagine anyone not wanting her. Not that I should talk, because it had been ages since I'd been on a date of my own. I was too poor and too annoyed to date right now.

"But you should do it soon, right? I mean, I'm sure that the sooner we file the better, because it's like we knew it was a mistake right away, you know?" I said. The fact that she hadn't done anything yet completely shocked me. Emma was always the one who paid her bills early and never liked leaving things until the last minute. Unlike me.

"Yeah," she said softly. "But I was thinking . . ." Emma trailed off, and finally looked up at me.

"What if . . . what if we didn't get it annulled? I mean, not right away." I stared at her, convinced I had heard her wrong. She could not be suggesting that we stayed in this mistake of a marriage. For what reason? Why would we do that?

"You want to *stay* married? Why?" I managed to say at last.

"Well, think about it," she said, using her hands because she had clearly thought about this and had been itching to tell me.

"What is there to think about? We can't just *stay* married, Em. Wouldn't we get in trouble?" She was freaking me out right now.

She leaned closer and she had a wild gleam in her eyes. "Why? Callyn, there's no marriage police. And consider that if we were married, it might benefit us." I shook my head, trying to get my thoughts to make sense.

"How?"

"Well, we could file our taxes jointly, it would help us financially, and we could share health insurance. There're all kinds of benefits. I looked them up." Of course she did. Emma proceeded to pull the list up on her phone and read it to me. My head spun with confusion and hearing too many words I didn't know the meaning of. What the hell was an estate tax?

"This is ridiculous, Emma. We can't do this. What would our parents say?" I shuddered at the thought. Not that my parents didn't adore Emma, because they did, but telling them that we'd gotten drunk married in Vegas and were staying married for the sweet financial perks might cause one or both of them to have a stroke.

"We don't need to tell them. I mean, how would they find out?" she asked. I gave her a look, because she had clearly lost her mind. Our friends knew already, and there was no hiding anything in the age of social media. "Okay, we'll cross that bridge when we get there. How about we try it? We try it for six months and then if you still want to get it annulled, I'll do it," she said.

I didn't know what to say, and I wasn't speechless very often. In fact, I couldn't remember the last I'd been speechless. A strange spluttering came from my mouth, like a car that wouldn't start. I couldn't make words, only sounds.

Emma shrugged. "Or we can annul it like we planned. No big deal. It was just an idea." She reached for my hands and clasped them. "It was just a silly idea." This really meant a lot to her and I had no idea why, but did that matter?

"I mean . . . yes, it's a completely off-the-wall idea. That's supposed to be *my* specialty." Emma didn't do things like this. Ever. That was what had me so confused. I was the one who should have come up with this. It was as if the world had flipped upside down and I was still trying to figure out how to stand.

"I know. But I was thinking about it and doing research

and well—I made a list and here we are." Even her off-the-wall ideas were researched and planned. So Emma.

I turned the idea over in my head as Emma waited and squeezed my hands so hard that I was worried about my circulation. It was as if she really wanted me to be on board with this. But why? It wasn't like I had a lot of money or something. My health insurance was bullshit, and I had no property. So the financial aspect was going to benefit me more than her. I couldn't understand what other compelling reason would make her want to do this, but it only took me a second to decide that her reasons didn't matter. This was Emma. My Emma. My best friend that I would walk through a hail of bullets for. Who I would walk miles over a path covered in fiery LEGOs for. Who I would do anything for. This was something she wanted and it didn't matter why. It only mattered that I would give it to her.

"Okay," I said. "What the hell? Let's stay married." Emma hugged me and I knew I'd made the right decision, even if I didn't know why I'd made it.

"What is wrong with us?" she said, laughing, her eyes sparkling. They were bluer in this light.

"No idea, but if this is wrong, I don't want to be right." I was *married*. I was married to my best friend. Emma was my wife. The word felt strange and forbidden and adult. Way too grown-up for me, or for us. It wasn't like I was going to come home from work and find her in the kitchen making a pot roast in heels and pearls. Granted, life wasn't a 50s sitcom, but still. We weren't *married* married, with sex and a house and a future and everything.

"I think we should celebrate," Emma said, bouncing up from the couch. I hadn't seen her this excited since they uncancelled her favorite space show. I waited on the couch as she bounded to the kitchen and came back with a tiny bottle of champagne and two glasses.

"I've had this in the fridge forever. I was saving it for, well, I don't know what for, but I think now is as good a time as any to drink it." She popped the cork and managed not to spill any on the floor.

"This is really weird, Em," I said, taking the glass from her. I was going to be good and sip this carefully. Moderation. That was what I needed right now, especially since alcohol was what got me into this. A few too many drinks and BAM, I have a wife.

"How about we just go with it?" she said, tapping her glass to mine.

"That's my line," I said. "Have I finally influenced you so much that you're stealing my personality?" I laughed, but I was a little serious. This new Emma was a stranger to me. Her eyes were wild with suppressed excitement.

"Are you going to be okay? I mean, are you stoked to have me as a wife or something?" I asked. She gulped some champagne and then put down her glass.

"No, Callyn, I'm just . . . I don't know. I feel like I've been going in circles for so long and then I finally decided to do what I wanted to do for the first time in my life and it's like I'm high on it. Everything seems different. I feel free, and it's making me a little loopy, I guess." I had noticed a change in her, definitely. Her shoulders weren't as slumped as they had been for years. She'd also stopped caring so much about what her parents thought, which I had been begging her to do, but she hadn't been able to do it until she was ready.

"I'm so happy for you, Em. You do seem different. I guess I'm adjusting too, but you can't become the impulsive one. That's my job." She grinned and the happiness radiated from her entire being. I loved seeing her this way. It made my heart feel like it was too big to stay in my chest without causing some internal damage.

"You're still going to be the impulsive one, Callyn. But

maybe now instead of listing all the reasons you shouldn't do the thing, I'll take your hand and do the thing with you." Why did that make me feel like I wanted to cry?

"I'll drink to that," I said, and we clinked our glasses again. "Wait, do I have to change my name? Do you have to change your name? Should we mash our last names together?" All kinds of thoughts hit me all at once.

"No, Callyn, you don't have to change your name. This is just temporary, remember? Just for six months. I mean, nothing is really going to be that different. Except you can get my health insurance, if you want." Emma had insurance through her new school. It wasn't great, but it was better than what I currently had from the hotel. I missed being on my parent's plan. I had had so much less to worry about back then and I didn't even appreciate it. I wanted to slap Past Callyn over that.

"Yeah, sounds good." That would be cool. Maybe I could even see a dentist. Being in your mid-twenties was wild.

"What would we change our names to, if we decided to do it? Could we be cool and do one where we put the letters of our last names together into a new name?" Emma laughed and we both typed the letters into our phones to see what we could come up with.

"What can we make with Stott and Vitali?"

"Stotali!" I said. "Uhhhhh, Vitott? Vott? Stali?"

"That last one sounds too much like Stalin."

"Right. Good point."

"How about Atlis? Ohhh, we could do Vitol."

"Now that one sounds too much like vitriol," I pointed out. Emma winced. We went through a few other options and finally settled on Volta.

"It sounds like a cool robot," Emma said. "Or a spaceship or superhero or something. I like it as a hypothetical last name."

"It's way cooler than Stott, that's for sure. I kind of want to take it anyway." I was completely joking, but Callyn Volta was such a badass name I was sad it couldn't be real. Callyn Volta wasn't the kind of person who put face wash on her toothbrush by accident. She wasn't the kind of person who put off returning a dress until the return window closed and lost money because she was too much of a dork to get herself to the store to return it. No, Callyn Volta wouldn't take shit from anyone, not even bitchy customers who yelled at you for things that weren't your fault.

"I could be Emma Volta, I think," Emma said.

"You totally could," I agreed.

"Emma and Callyn Volta. The Voltas." I laughed because it was all too ridiculous. Two weeks ago we were best friends and now we were The Voltas.

"We should get that monogramed on everything," I said.

"Definitely," Emma agreed and we both collapsed into laugher. I had no idea why it was so funny, but I couldn't get myself together. I laughed until there were tears streaming down my face and my ribs ached.

"Do you want to stay again?" Emma asked, as if that was even a question. I'd spent more time here in the past week than at my place. I always slept so much better at Emma's apartment.

"I think my roommates are trying to outdo each other with how loud they can be during coitus. Honestly, I kind of wish they would all go in one room and just all do it together so they could be done and I could get some peace and quiet," I said.

"Wouldn't that just be *really* loud, though?" she said. I shrugged.

"I guess. I just want them to stop banging all the time, or

at least do it more quietly. I mean, it's a slap in the face when you're not getting any." Emma always got awkward when I talked about sex and I tried not to, but sometimes I was just horny and frustrated and needed to vent to my best friend. I mean, she and I had zero secrets from each other, so I didn't get why she got squeamish about sex.

"Right," she said, staring at the bubbles in her champagne. There weren't many left; it had gone mostly flat.

"Emma, we're married."

"I know."

"No, we're *married*. That's a thing adults do. We're not adults. I mean, I'm not." I sure didn't feel like one. I was so bad at doing anything that adults were supposed to do. I was a complete and utter disaster of a person.

"You are. And you have me to help you with the difficult stuff. Who is the one who helps you detangle your taxes every year?" she asked, pouring more champagne into her glass. That would be Emma. She was my one-woman CPA, best friend, and advice-giver. Not that I always took her advice.

I pointed at her. "You. And who is the one to convince you to climb a mountain in the middle of the night so we can see a meteor shower?" She smiled softly at the memory. Sure, we'd thought we were going to get eaten the whole time by a bear, but once we'd gotten to the top of the small mountain, it had been completely worth it.

"That would be you, Callyn."

"Exactly. We need each other." I wasn't going to say that I needed her more than she needed me even though that was definitely true. I couldn't think of a difficult time in my life when she hadn't been there, when she hadn't been the person I leaned on when I thought all hope was lost. Emma was my everything. Maybe that was why I sucked at dating. Because I got so much of what I needed from Emma.

"You're my go home," I said. We had joked forever ago

about the saying "go big or go home," because we would both prefer to go home than go big, so we'd started calling each other our "go home" instead.

"Always," she said, throwing back the last of the champagne and making a face at how flat it was.

∽

ON SATURDAY all of the Bachelorette Babes (as we had dubbed ourselves) got together. We tried to meet at least twice a month to talk and rekindle our friendships. Since my family was meh, my friends were everything to me. I didn't have sisters or cousins or anyone to call when shit went down. I called Emma and then called the rest of the group.

It was my turn to pick our brunch place and I'd chosen a diner that looked greasy on the outside, but served things like kale and ginger smoothies and had an entire vegan menu on the inside. You had to love hipster Boston.

We had to wait for a while to get a table to seat all of us, and I wasn't prepared for the first question after we finally sat down and got menus.

"So, are you divorced yet?" Nova asked, not looking up from her menu. Sammi hit her on the arm.

"We agreed we weren't going to ask," she hissed, but her voice was so loud that we all heard her anyway. Sammi wasn't good at subtle.

"We're sitting right here," I said. Guess we were doing this now. Emma and I had talked about what to say and, even though we didn't want to lie to our friends, we decided it was for the best. We wanted to keep this thing between us. They could hear about it after everything was over.

"Yeah, we're getting it done. They have to process the paperwork and everything. Takes some time," Emma said, staring so hard at her menu that I hoped it didn't ignite from the power of her concentration.

"See? All set," I said, my stomach twisting with the lie. Emma and I had agreed that they wouldn't understand. They wouldn't get it.

"Well, that's good. You both kinda stole my thunder there," Lara said. I had already apologized about that, but I guess she was still a little salty about it.

"I promise not to announce a pregnancy at your reception, how's that?" I asked, and she tried to hide a smile.

She stuck her hand out and shook mine across the table. "Deal."

The topic of conversation moved back to Lara and her wedding, which was in a month. This was the first wedding I'd ever been in and I was already exhausted. Who knew being a bridesmaid was such a massive commitment? I hadn't realized, not until after I'd put the dress I couldn't afford on my credit card and then had to pay for alterations on top of it. Not to mention the time spent planning everything, and then there was the wedding itself. Rehearsal dinner, bridal brunch, wedding day, reception still to go. This was a marathon, not a sprint. Still, it was going to be a great time.

Lara's parents were loaded and they were going to spare no expense on their youngest daughter's wedding. She had three sisters and they'd all had grand weddings, so she was able to get what she wanted, because her sisters had. I wish my family was like that, or that I'd get a fraction of what they'd done for my sister, but you couldn't choose your family.

At least I was running this wedding marathon with Emma, and neither of us were the maid of honor. That position went to Lilly, Lara's next-oldest sister. She was also throwing Lara another bachelorette party, but that one involved a fancy hotel, tea, and board games. Lilly hadn't been up for the whole Vegas thing, which was understandable since she was pregnant. The Bachelorette Babes had agreed on two separate events, so we still had the second half of the party to get to in two weeks. Tired. I was already so tired and I hoped that none of my other friends were going to get married for an extremely long time, or at least had the decency to elope.

It was so strange to think about Lara getting married when I'd technically had a wedding of my own already. I just couldn't remember most of it.

"What are you thinking about?" Emma asked me, as I dug into my Garbage Plate, which was tater tots with cheese, sausage gravy, and two fried eggs on top. I didn't mess around when it came to brunch. I'd been tempted to get a Bloody Mary, but stuck with orange juice mixed with seltzer instead. Moderation, like an adult. I was learning.

"Moderation," I said. I didn't want her to know I was thinking about our forgotten wedding. I'd asked her a few times if she remembered anything and she always said that she didn't. Weird that neither of us could recall, but that was what happened when you got blasted in Vegas, I guess. I hadn't told her that I remembered one small moment, so I just pretended that the entire thing was a blank for me too.

"Interesting," she said. "In what way?" I looked up from my plate and at Emma.

"In every way. I think I should be less *impulsive*, don't you think?" I was teasing her, and it took a second for her to get that.

"That's probably a good idea," she said, nodding and her lips twitching from a suppressed smile.

"I think so." I swerved back into the larger conversation again as we chatted about Willa's latest dating escapades. For some reason that poor girl picked the worst people to date. It seemed like a cosmic joke at this point.

"How can you be so smart, but so bad at dating?" Emma asked.

"I don't knowwww," Willa said, dropping her head on her folded hands on the table. "Just because I'm good at tech doesn't mean I'm good at people." Willa's job was so techy that I didn't even know what it was, only that she worked at a company that made robots and I spent a lot of time telling her not to make them sentient and she would just roll her eyes at me.

This time her first date with a new girl had ended abruptly when the date's wife had walked into the bar they were at and was unaware that Willa's date was seeing people outside their marriage. Oops?

"So then I got a drink thrown on me, for some reason, and then I was wet and sticky, but the bartender gave me her number, so maybe it wasn't a total loss? Maybe I should just stop dating white people. No offense."

"None taken," Emma, Lara, and I said at the same time.

"I'm only half-white," Sammi said. We all laughed and agreed that the bartender was hot after looking her up online. That was a great meet-cute story, so I hoped it worked out.

Hearing horror dating stories made me glad to be single. Was I technically still single if I was in a sham marriage? I had to talk to Emma about that. How could we date other people if we were legally married? Not that I wanted to be dating, but you never knew when you might meet someone.

We sat around for a little while and then, since the sun was out, we agreed to head over to Boston Common and take a walk. The air was still full of summer, even though it was the beginning of September. The merry-go-round was still out, so I ran for it and Emma followed me, laughing. My rule was that I had to ride any merry-go-round I ever encountered, and as my best friend (and now my legal wife), Emma had to come with me. Lara, Willa, Nova, and Sammi also followed because they were good friends.

"I can't wait to be at Disney," I said as we waited in line near a bunch of children who gave us strange looks. I didn't even care. I was more than happy to be the adult going on the merry-go-round.

"I know," Emma said. "I feel like we've been planning it forever." As a group, we'd decided to take our annual Girl's Trip to Disneyworld next year and I couldn't be more excited. We usually just went to the beach for a few days, or to a cabin in the mountains, but next year we were doing it up. I was going to have to put most of it on my credit cards, but whatever. It was worth it.

"Yeehaw!" Nova yelled, swinging her arm above her head like she had a lasso.

"You are ridiculous," Sammi said, but she had a fond smile on her face.

"Do it with me," Nova said, leaning over her horse and kissing Sammi clumsily. "Come on, yeehaw with me!" Sammi let out a half-hearted yeehaw and then we all joined in and embarrassed ourselves.

"We're going to get banned from this merry-go-round," Sammi said, after the third round of yeehaws.

"Wouldn't be the first time," I said.

"And it won't be the last," Emma finished.

Chapter Four

So far, being married to Emma was pretty much exactly like not being married, except for every now and then it would hit me when I looked at her that she was legally my wife. There was a strange security in that kind of thing. Not ownership, because neither of us owned the other, more of a connection that made me feel safe. I couldn't put my finger on it, but I loved it, but I hadn't voiced it to Emma. I didn't know what she would think.

I had the interview at the co-working space, and I thought it went really well. The manager was non-binary, so we ended up talking about how important queer issues were to us, so that was a nice little connection.

The job sounded great and paid well, and I didn't think I'd have to deal with half the bullshit from the hotel. I left the interview feeling confident and the first person I messaged about it was Emma. She didn't get back to me right away, so I spent the entire ride on the T back to my apartment staring at my phone and waiting for her.

I'd taken the day off for my interview, and also to catch up on some things at home while my roommates were at their respective jobs. The place was a complete fucking disaster since I hadn't been around much.

First was the trash, then I tackled the dishes. My phone dinged with a new message and I quickly wiped my hands on a dishtowel before I picked it up. I was greeted with a picture of Emma smiling and giving me a thumbs up for nailing my interview. That was followed by a second pic with her sending me a kissy face.

Something in my stomach fluttered, and I couldn't help but smile. I sent her a kissy face in return and went back to the dishes.

A few hours later, the house was more livable and I had my second load of laundry in the dryer. I ordered sushi from my favorite place and hopped into bed with my freshly washed sheets to watch a Jane Austen movie for the thousandth time.

Of course I heard stomping feet on the stairs and braced myself for the noise. Moments later, there was a knock at my door.

"Yeah?" I said, and the door opened to reveal Eddie with a grim look on her face.

"Landlord is selling the house, so we have to be out in 30 days. Sorry." She turned around and shut the door to her room, leaving me sitting there in a state of shock. The fuck? I hopped out of bed and knocked on her door.

"What?" she said, whipping the door open and looking at me in irritation.

"Is that it? How do you know he's selling the place?" She rolled her eyes and sighed so long I thought it would never end before handing me a piece of paper. I scanned it and she was right. Our landlord was selling, and we had 30 days to be out, even though our lease wasn't up.

"Fuck," I said under my breath.

"Is that it?" Eddie asked, tapping her foot and crossing her arms.

"Yeah, I guess," I said, handing the paper back. I went back to my room in a daze. Our lease didn't end for several months, so I hadn't thought I would need to look for a new place this soon. I was completely fucked now. Thirty days wasn't a lot of time to find a new place. I wanted to cry.

I immediately called Emma, and she picked up right away.

"So, my landlord is a dick and I have to move in 30 days." Panic had started to set in and I thought of all the terrible things that could happen if I couldn't find an apartment.

"Move in with me," Emma said after a pause. "You can stay with me for a few months until you can find another place. It'll just be temporary. You can save some money and maybe get better roommates." Oh. I hadn't even thought of that. Fuckkkkk.

"Are you sure? I don't know how much rent I can do."

"Don't worry about it. You can help me with utilities. I'm not going to let my best friend be in a bad situation. I love you, Cal." Her voice broke a little as if she was getting emotional. So was I.

"Wow, that would be amazing. You don't have to do that."

"Yes, I do. You're my wife, remember? And my go home." Right. That.

"Okay. Okay. Are you sure? You'll have me there *all* the time. I'll sneak into the kitchen at two in the morning to make a charcuterie plate. I'll sing too loud in the shower." Emma laughed.

"I do know you, Callyn. I've known you my whole life. Nothing you could do is going to shock me."

I grinned. "That sounds like a challenge."

Emma groaned on the other end of the line.

"It'll be fine. You can move in now if you want. I can put most of my stuff in the basement." That didn't sound like a horrible idea. I mean, I'd have to pay rent here anyway, but the sooner I got out of here, the better.

"This weekend? Can we use your car?" I didn't have one, but Emma had a nice SUV that her parents got her when she went to college that would hopefully fit everything I needed to move.

"Sounds good. We'll be wives and roommates."

In spite of being best friends our whole lives, we'd never actually lived together. We hadn't gone to the same college, and we hadn't graduated at the same time, so it had never really worked out for us to be in the same apartment. Plus, our incomes were so different. She had parental support for her rent when she'd been younger. I'd had to scrape by on my own. I was sure we'd be able to live with one another with no problems.

"That's still really weird, Em," I said. "I don't know if I'll ever get used to it. I mean, I know it's only temporary." Emma sucked in a deep breath and was silent for a second.

"Right," she finally said. "Anyway, I'll clear out the spare room. Is there anything else you want to bring? I can move out some of my stuff and put it in storage so you can make this place more of a home, even if it's just for now." I'd always moved in with other people who already had furniture, so I didn't have much of my own. Just some lamps, a dresser, a bed frame, and a mattress. Pretty pathetic. I was going to be out of luck if I had to furnish my own place. I'd missed my chance to go "shopping" when all the college kids had moved out and put their shit on the street. You could outfit an entire house for free if you weren't worried about potential bedbugs.

"Uh, not really. My bed is pretty much shit. Yours is

nicer." Maybe this was a chance for me to start over with everything and maybe get some new stuff. I'd been getting by with the same crap since college.

"We'll pick out some new sheets for you, and you can decide how you want to arrange the room."

"Sounds good." All of the tension I'd felt when Eddie had dropped that particular bomb on me was gone. I was going to live with Emma. This was going to be fucking awesome.

~

"I SWEAR, I don't remember having this much stuff. I'm pretty sure some of it multiplied overnight," I said as we brought yet another box into Emma's living room. Well, I guess it was *my* living room now. Weird.

"Callyn, your stuff isn't tribbles." I squinted at her, wondering what the reference was from.

"Star Wars?" I asked. Emma gave me a sad look and shook her head as if she was terribly disappointed in me.

"Star Trek, original series." Right. She'd been begging me watch it forever, but I just hadn't gotten around to it. Maybe now that we lived together we could do a marathon. I could just picture it, the two of us cuddling up on her expensive couch and sharing a blanket and a giant bowl of popcorn topped with cotija, lime juice, cayenne, and butter. We had sleepovers all the time, but this would be different. We'd be together all the time.

"Is that the one with the sarcastic talking raccoon?" I asked, trying to remember. I had the worst time remembering character's names from different movies and shows.

"Oh my god, you did not just ask me that," Emma said, collapsing on a box with a groan.

"What?"

Emma shook her head.

"I'm going to make you flash cards and we're going to practice." I knew she wasn't joking. Emma had had to put up with me whispering "which one is he again?" so many times during movies, but she was always patient with me and explained who the character was so quietly that only I could hear her and no one else in the theater got mad.

"Fine, fine," I said, looking at all the boxes. I was finally free from my old place and my old awful roommates. There was going to be a lot less sex going on in this apartment, I'd wager. I mean, I wasn't going to be having any (except with myself), and I didn't think that Emma was either. My stomach rolled a little bit at the thought of Emma being that way with someone. It was weird to think about her that way, so I should probably stop.

"Callyn?" Emma asked, and I jumped at the sound of her voice and felt my face go red.

"Yup," I said, cracking the tape on the box and yanking out the first thing my hand could find, which turned out to be a candle.

"Where should I put this?" I said, not able to meet her eyes.

"Can I smell it? You know how picky I am about scents." She took the candle from me and inhaled deeply. "Oh, I like that. Smells like pine and campfire."

"Yeah," I said, still trying to snap myself back to normal. Emma took the candle from me and made some space on the mantle. Yes, she had a fireplace, which was sheer luxury in the city. She lit it and inhaled.

"Should we order some food? I'm starved." I was hungry too. Moving was exhausting work. My back was going to be angry tomorrow.

"Sure," I said, pulling some other items out of the box.

Emma pulled up the app to order and asked me what I was feeling like.

"Since it's your first night here, you get to choose where we order from." She handed me the phone and I scrolled through. Hell yeah, way better options than my old place.

"What are you thinking?" I didn't want to order from anywhere that she wouldn't like.

"I'm open to anything. Get what you want."

"What about . . ." I trailed off and scrolled. "Pasta? I need carbs." I added eggplant parmesan and garlic knots and Emma went for spaghetti and meatballs.

"And cake. We need cake," she pointed out.

"Always." I added two pieces of chocolate cake to the order and some seltzer waters.

Emma had cleared everything out of the room, except for the bed.

"Where is all your shit?" I asked.

"Uh, closet? Basement storage. Some of it is in my room now. Is this going to work for you?" This room was way bigger than my old bedroom. I wouldn't even know what to do with all this space. I'd lived in Boston so long that I'd forgotten what reasonable living quarters looked like.

"You didn't have to do that," I said again, but she waved me off and brought in another box.

"You're my best friend. I'd do anything for you."

"Plus, I'm your wife," I called to her, as I pulled some bedding from a box and started making the bed.

"Exactly!" she called back.

Chapter Five

"To our first night as roommates," Emma said, toasting us both. I'd gotten everything unpacked, and Emma had helped me add my decorative touches to the common spaces, which I hadn't asked for, but that she insisted on.

"Roommates, best friends, and wives," I said. That was a lot.

"Roommates, best friends, and wives," she repeated. We clinked our seltzer bottles together and reclined on the couch.

"A lot has happened in a short time," I said. "And we still have Lara's wedding extravaganza."

"I know. That's going to be a lot. It's a good thing I love her, because I wouldn't go through all this for just anyone," Emma said. I agreed.

"I'd be your maid of honor. You know, for the next wedding. The real wedding."

"I don't know if I want to get married. I mean, again, you know. Sober and all that," she said.

"Really?" I couldn't remember her ever saying anything like this. To be fair, I couldn't remember the last time we'd talked about marriage or anything related. I knew every single thing about her, but not this, for some reason.

"Yeah. I don't know."

"I can't really picture it either." That had never been my thing. I hadn't planned an entire destination wedding to Belize down to the rhinestone flowers on my dress. Sure, I'd wondered about weddings and marriage and kids, but I wasn't sure about anything.

"Anyway, I've got one wife already, so I'm not thinking about another one." She smiled and I couldn't help but smile back.

My wife. For now.

∼

"IT'S SO QUIET HERE," I said a while later. We'd devoured the cake and I was full and content. I hadn't realized that in my old place I hadn't really ever been able to fully relax. I'd always been stressed and annoyed and now it was like I could breathe freely.

Emma's hands wove through my hair and I closed my eyes.

"Are you saying I'm boring?" she said behind me.

"No. I'm saying this is nice. It's a relief." Almost as if this was meant to be.

"Good. I've wanted to ask you to move in for a while, but I wasn't sure how. I know that seems silly, since we share everything else. I don't know." I looked at her over my shoulder.

"I wanted to live with you too, but I knew I couldn't afford it." I was being blunt, but whatever. She knew how much money I didn't make.

"It's okay. I've got money." I knew she'd made decent money at her old job, but she was in school now and not working. I knew she wanted to get a part time job at some point, but was concentrating on getting a foothold in school first.

"I'm going to get another job, I promise. I had that interview and I'm just waiting to hear back. The pay would be great there. Plus, I'm working on my negotiating skills so I can start out with better pay," I said. I mean, I was going to try to do that. I'd only really practiced what I would say in front of a mirror. Things were totally different when I was in front of a boss or potential boss. At least I had a lot of incentive now to negotiate for more money. I couldn't be a financial burden on Emma.

"Hey, it's okay." She tucked her arm around me and pulled me back into her chest. "We've got this. Just you and me against the world."

"You and me," I said, yawning. It had been a long day, but I didn't want to go to bed just yet. I had a new book that I'd been saving for a few days to read and it was calling me.

"Do you mind if I read?" I asked.

"No. Why would I? This is your house. You can do whatever you want." I grinned at her.

"Does that mean I can rearrange the towels in the linen closet?" Her eyes narrowed.

"You can do whatever you want *except* that." I huffed and got up to grab my tablet. When I came back, she had her phone out.

"What are you looking at?" I said, peering over her shoulder.

"If you're gonna read, I'm going to read as well." We'd done this countless times before. Emma and I had spent so much time together that silence was always fine.

"What are you reading?"

"A nonfic about terrible rich people being terrible." Of course she was. "And you?" she asked.

"Screw that, I'm reading about ladies falling in love and banging. Why would you want to read anything else?" I couldn't imagine. Emma just laughed and went back to reading.

I cuddled up with her on the couch and turned my tablet on.

We read in silence until I was completely exhausted. I turned my tablet off and looked at Emma. She had leaned back on the couch and her eyes were closed. I studied her for a few moments before gently getting up.

"Hey, Em, you fell asleep." I stroked her shoulder and her eyes fluttered open.

"Hey," she said, a sleepy smile forming on her lips. My heart thumped against my chest in a frenetic beat. I'd seen her thousands of times before. Why was I feeling like this was the first time I'd noticed how completely beautiful she was? Her eyes were definitely blue tonight.

"Hey," I said. "We should probably go to bed. Or, at least, I'm going to. Remember, big day tomorrow." We were headed out to see one of Nova's art shows and then seeing a movie before having dinner at a new taco place that was opening, mostly because we wanted free tacos.

"You're right," she said, stretching her arms above her head. "Should we brush our teeth?" I held my hand out and helped her up from the couch and she followed me into the bathroom.

It didn't seem strange to brush our teeth together, since we'd done it hundreds of times before. I kept meeting her eyes in the mirror and smiling. Why did this moment feel so perfect? I wish I'd sucked it up and moved in with her years ago. Could have saved myself so much pain and aggravation. Sure, I might have been even more broke than I was now, but what did that matter?

Emma wiped some toothpaste from my mouth and laughed.

"Missed a spot."

"Thanks," I said, putting my toothbrush in its charger right next to hers. We had the same one, but different colors. Hers was white while mine was a sparkly blue.

"Goodnight wife," I said, laughing. Emma stared at me for a second and then leaned forward, giving me a kiss on the cheek.

"Goodnight wife," she said in my ear. I froze, completely unable to move. Unable to breathe. It was like my entire body stopped. As if that kiss had hit my internal pause button.

Emma left the bathroom and I finally inhaled. My skin burned where her lips had touched me. I put my hand to feel my cheek, just to make sure my skin was normal.

That gesture reminded me I needed to wash my face, but I didn't have the energy, so I just pivoted and went to the guest room—my room now. I heard music coming from behind Emma's door. She always slept with music on, just like I slept with the TV on. We both had anxious minds that needed something to distract them. On the surface, we seemed so different, but in so many small ways, we were just alike.

I got in bed, unable to stop thinking about the kiss. What was my deal? I was sure that Emma had kissed me on the cheek before. Hell, she'd seen me naked as fuck on so many occasions. What was a little cheek kiss? Puzzled, I stripped out of my clothes and went to bed in just a tank top and my undies. In the summer I slept naked, so I was definitely going to have to get a robe for when I had to go to the bathroom in the middle of the night. Didn't need to terrify Emma with my nudity.

I put on an old show and snuggled under my new covers,

wishing I had a pet of some kind to snuggle. A dog, a cat, I didn't really care. Just something cute and furry to keep me company and sleep in my bed. Of course, with all my luck I'd get an animal that would hate cuddling and would destroy all my shit. Plus, I didn't think Emma would go for it. Pets were messy and complicated things.

I tried my meditation app, but my brain wouldn't empty out the way I wanted it to. I couldn't push away the thoughts and just focus on my breath, and it was getting really annoying.

All I wanted to do was relax and sleep, but my brain wasn't letting me do that. I tried again and again to let those thoughts go, but they wouldn't leave me alone. They weren't even thoughts, really. Not anything fully formed; just little bits of *something* that kept whizzing by.

A few minutes later, there was a knock at my door. It could only be one person, because a murderer probably wouldn't knock.

"Yeah?" I asked, and the door opened a crack and Emma poked her head in.

"I can't sleep. I don't know why. Can I hang out with you for a little bit?" I scrambled to sit up.

"Uh, sure." She sat on the end of my bed, crossing her legs and grabbing one of my pillows to hold onto.

"Something on your mind? You should use my meditation app," I said. Not that it had been working for me.

"I'm just thinking about all this change and how okay with it I am. You know me, I don't like it when things are different." Yes, I did know. I'd been witness to more than one of Emma's breakdowns when we were kids and something was different. It was one of the reasons I was so shocked when she actually quit her job and enrolled in school. I had the feeling she'd had a few breakdowns over that, but she'd hidden them from me.

"I know, but you're doing so awesome. I'm really proud of you and so grateful that I'm here. I can't tell you how wonderful it is that I'm not listening to Eddie banging her horrible boyfriend and him asking if he could jizz on her face." We both shuddered.

"You're not going to hear that here, that's for sure," Emma said with a little laugh. "You can bring people here, you know. If you wanted to. This is your apartment and if you wanted to bring someone home, you could. Just so you know." Her voice was quiet and she pulled at a thread on my pillow, twirling it around her finger once it came free.

"Oh, okay. I mean, same for you? Not that you need my permission or anything." Why did talking about dating always get so weird with Emma? Why couldn't we talk about this kind of stuff?

"I mean, I'm probably not going to be picking anyone up anytime soon because it would be a little weird if you bumped into her and I had to introduce you as my best friend and wife."

"Fake wife, but I'm not sure if that would make a whole lot of sense to anyone but us," I said. Hell, it didn't make sense to me and I was living it.

She lapsed into silence and I could tell that she was working something through in her mind, but she didn't want to say it out loud yet. I waited until I couldn't take the suspense anymore.

"Something else on your mind, Em?" Sometimes getting at what was really bothering her out was like trying to reach a grape that had rolled under the fridge.

"Nothing," she said, putting the pillow back and getting up. I definitely wasn't still thinking about that cheek kiss from earlier and if she was going to do it again when she said goodnight. Not at all.

"Okay. Um, goodnight? Unless you want to snuggle a

little." I moved over and held the blanket up so she could climb in with me.

"No, that's okay. I should get back to my own bed," she said. I didn't know why that was so disappointing, but it was. Almost as if I'd been rejected, but that was silly. She was going to bed, like I should be doing. What did I expect, that she was going to climb in and sleep the whole night with me?

"Goodnight, again," she said, backing out of the room and giving me a little wave. No second kiss for me then.

"Goodnight," I said, as she shut the door. "I wish I had a puppy."

"What?" she said, opening the door again. I guess she'd heard me.

"Nothing, goodnight." She gave me a look, but I waved her off. "Going to sleep now."

"Me too." The door closed and I lay back and stared at the ceiling for a moment.

My cheek still tingled from where her lips had touched it.

~

I DIDN'T GET much sleep, but I woke up in a great mood because I was going to spend the day with Emma, my favorite person. I also awoke to the smell of bacon, which was the best way to wake up, in my opinion.

I stretched and opened my eyes to an unfamiliar room. For a moment, I had forgotten that I lived with Emma.

Yawning, I headed out and found her in the kitchen standing over a pan of bacon, dancing to Dolly Parton. What was a girl to do but grab a spatula and sing into it like a mic with her? She burst out laughing, and I jumped away from the bacon pan so I didn't get splattered by hot grease.

"Good morning to you too," she said, tipping the bacon onto a plate that was covered in a paper towel. "I've got bacon and biscuits with eggs and cheese if you want. Oh, and there's strawberries." I had definitely leveled up my breakfasts since moving here. "My bacon," she said in that creepy voice, and I shuddered.

"You didn't have to do that," I said, brushing her shoulder with my hand and then backing off when she jumped and turned the music down so we could hear each other. Emma moved away from me and started getting out silverware.

"I love making breakfast on the weekends. During the week it's toast and coffee, but weekends are made for elaborate breakfasts, in my opinion." I couldn't argue with her there. Plus, I got to eat said breakfast.

Emma loaded up our plates and we sat on stools at the kitchen island.

"It's so quiet here," I said. Even the noise from the street was peaceful, unlike at my old apartment, which was on a main street and only a block away from both a hospital and a fire station. Sirens, all the freaking time. I'd never gotten used to the wailing at all hours of the day and night.

Emma set her fork down and sipped at her orange juice. "I'm glad you like it, and I'm glad you're here. I keep forgetting that I don't live alone anymore." I couldn't remember ever living alone. I'd been surrounded by family or roommates my whole life. I'd probably start talking to the walls or something if I was alone that much.

"Can't relate, but it sounds nice."

"It was, but it got pretty lonely sometimes. I thought about getting a cat or something, but I'd have to get one of those hairless ones and they're so ugly." I gasped and dropped my fork dramatically.

"Excuse me, hairless cats are the ugliest little cute things in the world. Let's get a hairless cat!" I clasped my hands in a begging posture. I had never wanted a hairless cat before this moment but now I wanted one more than anything. Impulsive Callyn strikes again.

Emma made a face. "Ew, no. You may think they're cute, but I will never come around to them. We might look at a different kind of pet, though. Do you want to get a pet? You mentioned something about it last night." Yeah, she definitely heard me.

I stood up so fast that I knocked the stool over in my excitement. "Um, yes? Having a pet would make my life a hundred percent less sucky." Emma laughed and munched on her bacon daintily. I'd eaten mine first because it was the best part of breakfast. Plus, Emma always got the good bacon. Thick-cut, with plenty of spice.

Emma rolled her eyes. "That seems like an exaggeration, but if you want to look at the shelter, we can. I don't think we should get anything with scales, or that requires a heat lamp. I also don't like the idea of having to feed something mice." I agreed with that.

"Can we get a puppy? You know I've always wanted a dog." My parents would never let me have one because I wouldn't be "responsible" enough to take care of it. My older sister got a fucking horse for her birthday. Granted, it was a rental horse, but still. They always said they loved us the same, but then they would do shit like that and make it pretty obvious they were liars.

Emma pinched the bottom corner of her lip between her teeth. That meant I was wearing her down. "I don't know, Cal. That seems like a lot. Are you up for puppy training? I'm going to be in school a lot and if you get a new job . . ." she trailed off when she saw the pout on my face.

"Please?" I begged, pushing my lip out for maximum pout. I knew exactly what buttons to push to get my way with her ninety-nine percent of the time.

Emma narrowed her eyes and slowly shook her head. It was working.

"You're a real menace, you know that?" I smelled victory. It smelled like thick-cut bacon.

"Yes, but I'm a menace who's getting a puppy with my best friend-slash-fake wife." Emma sighed and rested her head on the table.

Her voice was muffled when she spoke. "This is going to blow up in my face, I know it." I let out a little victory squeal and grabbed both of our plates.

"I'll deal with the dishes," I said. It was the least I could do. I rinsed them off and put them in the dishwasher before starting on the pans she'd cooked with, making sure to turn the music back up again. Dancing made everything better, even dishes, so I started to boogie and sing at the same time. I knew all the words to all the Dolly.

"We should get going," she said, grabbing the frying pan from me and quickly drying it with a dishtowel so she could hang it up again on the little rack above the kitchen island.

I dried my hands and turned to face her. Emma stepped close to me with a strange look on her face. She reached toward me and wiped something from the same cheek she'd kissed last night.

"You had some soap on your face," she said, her voice so soft that it was barely above a whisper.

"Thanks," I said loudly. I couldn't move. An alarm on Emma's phone went off and we both jumped a mile. Emma had alarms set for just about everything, including getting ready to go out. All that organization would do the opposite and stress me the fuck out, but I guess I was going to be living with it now. Maybe her habits would finally rub off on me?

"Time to get dressed," she said, looking up from the phone before she turned around to head to her bedroom. I leaned back against the sink for a second. I needed the support. My heart was still racing, and it wasn't because of the alarm. What was going on with me? Was I having some sort of breakdown? What was going ON?

~

EVENTUALLY I GOT my shit together (as much as I ever could) and went to my room to get ready. I wanted to look nice for Nova's latest show, so I picked out my favorite floral romper that made me feel like I needed to frolic everywhere, and paired it with wedges and loosely braided my light brown hair. Just a little bit of color on my cheeks and brows completed everything.

I was the first one in the living room and was messing around on my phone when Emma emerged from her room. I dropped my phone on the floor with a thunk. I was too busy staring at her to worry about the potential of a screen crack.

"You, uh, look—" I couldn't think of a word. I'd forgotten how to word. I swear I'd forgotten how to breathe.

Emma's brows knit together in concern. "You okay?" she asked, brushing her fingers down the dress to smooth nonexistent wrinkles in the tropical print dress. It had a thigh slit that fluttered open when she moved and had large pink flowers on a white background.

"Yeah, fine," I said, finally picking up my phone. No screen cracks. "I've just got leg envy. You look fantastic." I stood on my own shaking legs and followed behind her as she grabbed her bag and keys from the table near the door. Right. I needed those things also. I slung my bag over my shoulder and joined her in the hallway.

I caught a whiff of orange from her hair as she locked the door. She must have sprayed it in the bathroom. Her dark ringlets were loose and pulled back on one side with a few bobby pins. Effortless casual elegance. I could never.

"You look *really* good," I said, at a loss for anything else.

"Well, thank you. You look really great too. I've always loved that romper on you." I did a little curtsy and ended up tipping over a little. On my best days, I wasn't the most coordinated.

"Guess that needs a little work before I meet the queen. Do you still have to curtsy to the queen? Is that a thing? Or do you just sort of bow over her hand? I'm sure someone's written an article online about this," I babbled as we headed down the stairs.

"I'll look up some tutorials for you, just in case," Emma said.

∽

NOVA'S GALLERY was only a few stops on the train away from our apartment, so we didn't bother to take a car. Of course I was limp and sweaty by the time we got to the gallery and climbed the stairs. Emma looked slightly windswept and incredible. I pulled a tissue out of my bag and blotted my face. Ugh.

"Is my hair okay?" I asked, using my phone to check the damage that the Boston wind had done. Most days there was no point in styling because it was just a waste of time when you stepped out the door.

"Yeah, it's perfect," she said, tucking a few pieces behind my ear, her finger lingering a little before she stepped through the doorway into the gallery. I shook myself a little and swallowed before I followed her.

The show was a joint venture between Nova and two of her friends. Nova was the painter, her friend Skye did photography, and the third member, Dierdre, did incredible wire sculptures. I always joked they should form a band and conquer the music world too.

Emma pressed a plastic glass of cheap wine into my hand and I looked for both Nova and the snack table. I found the former first.

"Hey, thanks for coming," she said, breezing over and giving us both hugs. She was dressed to impress in a gold sequin tube dress with her hair pushed back with a gold headband and gold shadow on her lids. Literal goddess.

"Are you the art?" I asked, and she laughed.

"You're ridiculous and I love you. Okay, I have to go do my thing, but I hope you enjoy, there's food in the back." Nova flitted away to chat and talk with Serious Art People.

"Shall we browse?" Emma asked, and we started on the left side of the room, moving from painting to sculpture. They had gotten inspired by the stories of Black women and children who were homeless, and just scanning the show was like a punch in the gut. Incredible. A part of the proceeds of the sale of any of the art went toward various charities helping black women and children afford housing and other necessities.

"I feel like I'm not smart or worthy enough for this," I said to Emma.

"Shhh, we don't have to get it. We just have to appreciate it and be supportive. Art is subjective." Right. We made it to the back and headed for the food table.

"Now *this* is a work of art," I said, picking up a little spinach and artichoke tart.

"Don't say that too loud," Emma whispered, getting me a little plate to pile my snacks on. I did some serious damage with the hors d'oeuvres before getting back to the other side of the show. I started to appreciate the art more once I had food and one glass of wine in me. The power in the work was so intense, I had to wipe a few tears at Nova's piece featuring a mother holding her child sitting on a sidewalk outside a shelter. I shared a look with Emma and there were tears in her eyes too. We weren't the only ones.

"Our friend is really talented and I feel like a loser in comparison," I said, when we'd reached the final piece that was a sculpture Dierdre had made that was simply called *Joy* that was a child standing with her face upturned, her eyes closed, and a sweet smile on her face.

"You say that at every one of Nova's shows," Emma pointed out. "You have your own talents, Callyn. So what if you can't capture something like this?" She pointed to a painting of a woman looking out of a dirty window, her chin resting in her hand.

I put my hands up and looked around. "What are my talents? Where are they? Besides always spilling food on myself?" I pointed to the spot on my romper. I'd been as careful as I could, and yet.

Emma pulled me aside so we were alone in a deserted corner. "Listen to me, Callyn, you're the *best* best friend someone could ask for. You're loyal as hell, you always find the joy in any situation, you're funny as fuck, you make the best grilled cheese sandwiches ever, you're good at stacking a dishwasher, you have a remarkable knowledge for random bird species, you always know how to make me feel better when I feel like shit, and you look really, really good in a romper. Is that good, or should I keep going?" I was rendered speechless. I'd been at a loss for words so many times today.

I sputtered a few times. Emma stood so close to me that it was hard to breathe. "Um, that's good for now but I might want some more later?"

"How about some more wine?" she asked, and I nodded. She went back to the food table as I tried to compose myself.

"You doing okay?" Nova was back with Sammi on her

arm. Sammi was also dressed in gold, with velvet pants and a matching jacket and black boots.

"You both look incredible," I said, while I waited for Emma to come back. Nova was so tall, and Sammi was petite, but they fit together so perfectly. Standing next to them made you almost high on the love they shared for one another.

"We do, don't we?" Nova said, kissing Sammi's head.

"I told you these pants were a good idea. You said I'd never have anywhere to wear them, and look at me now." Sammi twirled, and Nova tilted her head to the side.

"I never said you wouldn't have anywhere to wear them, babe. If I remember correctly, I complimented the way your ass looks in them because hell yes," she said, and they both laughed. I felt like I was intruding and it was a relief when Emma returned, this time with more wine and a plate of mini cakes.

"Oh, *you* are the best," I said. It would take me about a thousand years to list all of Emma's talents. Right now, those talents involved knowing that I needed cake and bringing it to me.

"I try," she said as I shoved one of the little cakes into my mouth. It had blackberry jam in the center and when I bit down some of it squirted down my chin. Emma smiled and mopped my chin with a napkin she pulled out of nowhere.

"I'm a mess," I said, taking the napkin and finishing the job myself. "Am I good?"

"You two are so cute," Sammi said, putting her head against Nova's arm. Nova dwarfed Sammi by almost a foot, so Sammi couldn't put her head on Nova's shoulder without a stepladder.

"What?" I asked, as Emma tossed the napkin and ate one of the cakes much more daintily than I did, and without spilling anything on herself. Unfair.

Nova nudged Sammi and gave her a look.

"You two are so cute. As friends. You know," Sammi said.

"Riiiiiight," I said, drawing the word out. What was she talking about? I looked at Emma, but she was concentrating real hard on the two cakes left on the plate.

"On that note, I have to go make a speech," Nova said, and she joined Skye and Dierdre, calling for everyone's attention.

"Thank you all for coming to our show," Nova said. I glanced at Sammi, who was glowing with so much pride, she was almost incandescent. Fuck, I wanted that.

Something made me look at Emma and I found her watching me with an intensity that made my cheeks go red. So distracted by her, I missed Nova's speech and was a little late in raising my glass. Oops. Distraction had replaced Jean as my middle name today.

～

WE HUNG around for a little while longer and I had a few more cakes before we headed out to the movies.

"Are you even going to want popcorn after all that?" Emma asked as we hopped on the train to get to the theater.

"Hell yes, and a giant drink, but I'm hoping there will be a dead zone where I can pee, because there's no way I'm making it through this entire thing without going at least once." Why didn't long movies come with an intermission, like plays? It was so annoying.

"I'll just let you know what you missed when you come back. No hurting your kidneys," she said.

"That's why you're the best," I said. She really was. "And I'll do the same for you. That's what best friends and fake wives are for."

I ENDED up having to pee twice during the movie, and Emma got shushed the second time I came back when she told me what had happened. I glared at the person and thought about dumping ice on their head, but refrained.

"I can't believe you ate all that popcorn," Emma said as I dumped the empty box in the trashcan after the credits rolled.

"I think there's enough sodium to completely preserve my body in the event of my death, so who's winning here?" I shot back.

Emma shook her head. "Are you even hungry? Should we wait a little while before we have dinner?" I was pretty full from everything still.

"Yeah, you wanna just walk around?" She agreed and we left the theater to wander up and down the street, stopping in any stores that looked interesting. Of course I dragged her into a bookstore and she followed me around as I piled paperbacks in her arms. I also grabbed a Blind Date with a Book, because why not? It was an easy impulse to indulge in that didn't hurt anyone.

"You should get one," I said, as I looked at the descriptions on the wrapped books. You couldn't see the title, author, cover, or blurb, but someone had written a sparse description and you picked your choice based on that. I loved it.

"This looks cool," she said, nodding at one on the second shelf. I picked it up for her and we both walked to the counter to check out.

"I've got this one," I said, adding her book to my stack. I winced at the amount, but books were better than something else I might blow my paycheck on.

"Shit, I should have brought my backpack," I said, realizing too late that I would have to carry all these books back home. "I think I might have made a mistake."

"I tried to tell you. We can take a car home if you want." Emma took one bag and I took the other as the cashier handed me the receipt.

"I think we also might need some more bookshelves if you're going to keep buying books," Emma said, as I held the door for her. She had a point. I did tend to buy a lot of books. More so now that I had an actual place to store them. I'd crammed my tiny room full of as many as I could and it was a disaster. Wobbly piles everywhere, but I knew which book was in which stack.

"That would be great. But you'll have to tell me when to stop because without any regulation, I'm liable to fill the entire apartment and then there will be no room for the puppy." Emma groaned.

"I forgot about the puppy. I don't think I'm up for that today."

"Speaking of that," I said, reaching out and stopping her from walking, "can we get tacos and then go to the shelter? Just to look?" I tried batting my eyelashes for good measure. That was supposed to work, right?

"Why are you blinking like that?" Emma asked, looking concerned.

"I was batting my eyelashes," I said, a little miffed. Guess I hadn't done it right.

"Yes, we can get tacos and then go to the shelter, but just to *look*," Emma said. "Why do I always feel like the mean mom in this friendship?"

"I mean, you could just give in to my demands and then you wouldn't have to." Emma snorted.

"You're impossible," she said.

"Is that one of my talents?"

"Definitely," she said.

We reached the taco place and I sat down with the books as Emma got our food. I couldn't stop thinking about potentially getting a puppy. I was a five-year-old, apparently. Emma was quiet.

"You okay?" I asked.

"Yeah, just thinking." She didn't sound like she was thinking about anything good.

"We don't have to get a puppy if you don't want to. Please don't give in to my demands just because you're my best friend. That's not good for either of us." All my words came out in a rush. The last thing I wanted was for Emma to cave to something she didn't want just because she wanted to make me happy. We'd end up resenting each other and I couldn't handle that. Not a good way to go about a fake marriage, or a real one. This was good practice for the real thing I might have someday.

She shook her head. "No, no, I'm actually excited about the puppy, now that I've had some time to think about it. If we find the right one, of course. We might want to do some research on breeds and so forth before we pick one, though. We can't just pick the first one that's cute, no matter how much we want it."

"Why not?" I shoved an entire tortilla chip in my mouth and crunched down on it.

"Callyn. Because we might end up with a dog that will be massive when it grows up and completely destroy our entire apartment because it needs a yard to run around in?" Oh, yeah, good point. I hadn't thought about that.

I put my hand up to stop her. "Okay, okay. You're right. We'll agree to look today, and do our research before we commit. So we'll do the opposite of what we did when we got married."

I paused for a second. "Did you ever remember

anything? About how it happened?" Emma shook her head and then dropped her taco on her plate, where it shattered.

"Nope," she said, staring down at the sad remains of a once-great taco that had caved to pressure.

"Me neither," I lied. "Guess we'll never know whose idea it was. So far, being married has been fine. I mean, I think living together has been more of an adjustment than the marriage stuff."

"True," she said, giving up on trying to put the taco back together and going at it with a fork.

We finished our food mostly in silence, and I didn't like it. There was still something bothering her and I wanted to know what it could be. Maybe seeing cute puppies would perk her up?

Emma and I took a car to the shelter, and I couldn't help but squeal with excitement as we walked in. Emma took the lead and I followed behind her, hauling the books. Why had I bought so many?

"Yes, we're considering getting a dog and we'd like to see what you have, as well as know what the process is like?" Emma said to the woman with the curly bleach-blonde in a polo shirt behind the tall counter. Lots of barking came from a room off to the right and I could sense the dogs were just out of reach. So close.

The woman smiled and looked at me, hunched over with two bags of books. I should have gotten one about raising dogs, probably. I tried to give her my most-responsible smile. She glanced back at Emma.

"Okay, well you need to fill out an application, which you can do now, and we'll take you back and you can see the dogs we currently have for adoption. Were you looking for more of an older dog, or a puppy? Several litters were just dropped off last week, so we're a little desperate for homes right now." I wanted to cry when she said that.

"Think of all the poor babies," I said to Emma, as she started filling out a form on a clipboard and the woman took a phone call.

"Let's get the form filled out first," Emma said. "You need to do one too." I picked up a clipboard and started filling it out. "Oh, it asks if we're married. We can say yes." I checked the box and my stomach felt like it was going down a roller coaster. My life was so weird right now.

Emma and I finished the forms and chatted with Deb, the volunteer.

"I think we definitely want a puppy?" I said, and Emma agreed. "We have a pretty decent apartment, but maybe one on the medium or smaller sized. Not too hyper?" Deb nodded and took us down the hallway as the rows of dogs barked or wiggled or tried to hide.

"I'll show you a few of the puppies we've got right now, there's quite a few to choose from. We're not totally sure on the breeds since they're mutts, but we can estimate what size they might be when they're grown." That sounded fine and I had the sudden urge to take Emma's hand. As if we had to play pretend married in front of Deb. Like she wouldn't give us a puppy if we didn't show that we were really a couple. What nonsense.

Deb came to the end of the hallway and took us through another door that had smaller cages stacked on top of one another.

"Oh my god, look at them," I said as we were assaulted by little puppy barks.

"We can't take them all. We can only take *one*," Emma said in my ear, but she was grinning too.

"I know, but that won't stop me from wanting to take them all," I whispered back.

Someone called Deb back to the front so she told us to

look around and then she'd come back and we could take out any puppy we were interested in.

Emma and I strolled up and down the rows of cages. I was waiting for a connection to hit me. When I met our dog, I would know.

"Hello precious babies," I said as they wiggled and cried for attention and tried to lick me through the bars of the cage. There were signs all over the place saying not to put your fingers near the cages and I decided to err on the side of caution.

"Hi sweetheart. Aren't you adorable?" I heard Emma say and turned to see her making eye contact with a little black shape that was wiggling so hard I couldn't get a visual handle on how big it was.

I joined her and made eye contact with the black blur, which turned out to have blue eyes almost exactly the same shade as Emma's. The puppy stopped moving and stared at me and that was it. My moment. Our eyes locked and then the puppy started the wiggling again and Emma put her arm around me.

"What about this one?" she asked.

Deb returned and we both pointed at the black puppy. "That one."

Deb smiled. "Oh, he is a sweetheart. Such pretty eyes. He's the runt of the litter, so I think that's why no one has taken a fancy to him yet. He's either energetic or sleeping, and he certainly seems to like you." Deb pulled him out of the cage and set him down on the floor where he was so excited we couldn't get a hold of him. Emma and I both got down on the floor and he jumped up and licked our faces, going back and forth as if he couldn't decide who he loved more.

"Yes, you are a good boy," Emma said.

"The best boy," I told him. He yipped in happiness and spun in circles.

Deb chuckled. "Looks like he's picked you. What do you think?" I shared a glance with Emma and it was one of those moments where we didn't need words.

"He's ours," I said. I didn't even think to ask what kind of dog he was.

"I know we weren't planning on taking a dog today, but look at him," I said to Emma as Deb went to process our paperwork.

"I know," Emma said as the puppy ran to a corner and grabbed a squeaky toy, bringing it back and dropping it at her feet, looking up expectantly. He really did have extraordinary eyes. His face was a little smushed, but his ears were enormous.

"At least he won't need a lot of grooming, since he has short hair," Emma said.

"Right. Oh look, he's got a heart on his belly." The puppy had rolled onto his back and was looking at both of us as if we knew what he expected us to do.

"He does," Emma said, scratching his belly as his eyes closed in bliss.

Deb came back and told us that we'd been approved and gave us a bunch of information about vaccinations and food and I let Emma handle most of that since she was the one who would actually remember to make the appointments with the vet and keep them.

Since we didn't have any supplies for our new addition, we bought a bag of food, a carrier, and more toys than the puppy would ever need from the shelter.

"Here's some information on local trainers and classes," Deb said as she put our new addition into a carrier for the trip home.

Emma and I called a car and I worried the driver would be unhappy about the puppy, but the woman who came to pick us up exclaimed how cute he was and helped us get everything in the car and gave us tips on the ride back to our apartment.

"We have a dog," Emma said, as we walked through the door. We had to make a few trips to get everything upstairs, but once we did, I set the carrier down.

"So, I think we should puppy proof this place before we let him out? Maybe we can put him in the bathroom for now," I said, as if I knew what I was talking about.

Emma agreed, so we moved everything in the bathroom out of chewing range and then went like tornados through the rest of the apartment, trying to make sure we moved anything he might get into, or gnaw on.

"I mean, a little bit of chewing is going to happen. I just have to accept it. Chew marks will give our furniture character," Emma said as I spread the toys out on the living room rug.

"You know what we forgot to get? Those wee-wee pads. And maybe we should get a gate and section it off before we let him have the run of the place," I said. Crap. He was going to pee all over this place.

Emma stood up. "Right. Okay. I'm going to go get those and you stay here with him. He might be hungry or thirsty, so fill up his bowls." Emma was already a nervous dog mom and it was cute as hell. I went into the bathroom and found our new baby crying, but as soon as he saw me, he skidded over and put his paws on my legs.

"Hey, baby. I'm sorry we had to put you in here. That wasn't very nice, was it?" Not wanting to leave him again, I picked him up and just carried him to the kitchen with me as I washed out his new bowls and filled one with water and the other with food.

Emma came back a while later hauling a metal cage and a giant bag of pee pads.

"Okay, let's set this up. How's he doing?" I looked up from my position on the floor where he was asleep in my lap and making soft snoring noises.

"Help," I said. "He's so cute and I don't want to move him." Emma laughed and joined me on the floor.

"What are we going to call him?" she asked.

"I've been thinking about that," I said, stroking his velvety ear. "What about Vegas?"

"I love it. Is that your name?" Emma said to the sleeping puppy whose eyes shot open and he abandoned me to let Emma know how much he had missed her.

"Is your name Vegas?" she asked him, and he barked twice. "That sounds like a yes."

"Good enough for me," I said, watching as Emma cooed and fussed over Vegas.

We set up a little puppy corner in the living room complete with blankets and toys and his food and water and wee-wee pads.

"I've never trained a dog before," I said.

"Neither have I," Emma said, as Vegas christened the floor before I could rush him to the wee-wee pad.

"This is going to be interesting," I said.

"To the internet!" Emma said, raising her hand as if she had a saber and was charging into battle.

"You look up potty training, I'll look up how to keep him from chewing on everything."

"Deal," Emma said.

Vegas chomped on a squeaky toy, as if agreeing with us.

What had we gotten ourselves into?

Chapter Six

A FEW HOURS (and used pee pads) later, we had to decide what to do with Vegas while we slept.

"If we let him sleep in our beds, then he's going to pee in them, I hope you know that," Emma said. She was being the mean mom again.

"But if we leave him out here by himself, he'll be sad and lonely. We can't do that to him. It's his first night." I had Vegas in my lap and he was asleep again. I'd taken him out of the little pen and brought him to sit on the couch with us after he'd given me one too many looks of sadness from puppy jail.

"Okay, so what are we going to do? Sleep in the puppy pen?" She said it like she was joking.

"Perfect! Just for tonight. We can start training him tomorrow. You have all the instructions." She'd already made a bulleted list of all the steps and printed it out. We were going to start tonight because neither of us wanted to be cleaning up wee-wee pads forever. As soon as he woke up, we were going to take him outside and wait for him to do his thing, then reward.

As if he'd heard me, Vegas lifted his head and stared at Emma before getting up and going over to her.

"Time to go outside, sweet boy. Do you want to come with me?" she asked me.

"Of course I do. You're not in this alone. I can be responsible too," I said, a little defensive.

"No, I know. We're in this together, because I'm not raising this boy on my own." I laughed at how much she sounded like a mother just then.

"I'm not leaving you, or our baby. Am I?" I said to Vegas, who licked my hand. Emma snapped a leash on his new collar (we still needed tags with our numbers on them), and we took him outside and down the sidewalk.

"Okay, now we wait," Emma said as Vegas went wild sniffing everything and wiggling all over the place, running away and then coming back to check if we were still there.

It only took ten minutes, but he did his business and then was properly rewarded and told what an incredible, handsome, genius boy he was, along with a treat that he munched on before we went inside.

"Good job," I said, high-fiving Emma.

"I think we're going to be good moms. Dog moms," she clarified. I wanted to ask her if she ever thought about upgrading to human children, but that was another thing we didn't really talk about.

I wasn't having them anytime soon since doing that would probably require a donor and lots of planning, *if* it was something I decided I wanted.

Emma and I set up blankets and pillows in the living room and settled Vegas in between us as we watched a new episode of a show. He seemed to alternate between off-the-charts energy and being completely asleep. I could understand that on a deep level.

"Do you love him?" Emma asked, as I stroked Vegas's head.

"I do. He's perfect."

"He is, isn't he?" she said, smiling down at him.

"No regrets about getting him, even though it's going to complicate our lives?" I asked.

Emma sighed. "I mean, in less than a month I picked up a wife and a roommate and a dog. What more could I want?" Sounded like a pretty great life to me, after things being pretty shitty for a long time.

"How about a million dollars?" I said.

"Yes, that would be nice, but this is pretty great too, being here with you and Vegas. And chips." She held up a bag that we'd been passing back and forth. The trick had been keeping the bag and its contents away from Vegas, which was a challenge, but fun. He'd only been ours for a few hours, but I already couldn't imagine life without him. Seriously, I would stand in front of a runaway train if it threatened him.

We took him out again, and this time it took nearly a half hour before he went potty, and I almost fell asleep waiting. The three of us settled onto the pile of blankets and pillows and I snuggled closer to Emma, with a drowsy Vegas cradled between us.

"How is he so perfect?" I asked.

"I don't know. But he's ours." He was. Ours.

∼

I WOKE up in the middle of the night to Vegas whining. Emma was asleep, so I took him out and did the rewarding. When I got back, Emma was awake.

"He had to make a tinkle," I said, and then cringed at myself. "I hate that I just said that. Who am I, my grandmother?"

Emma smiled drowsily as I set Vegas between us. He flopped down with a sigh and she kissed his head.

"We should go back to bed," I said.

"Or we could stare at him for a few hours."

"Yeah, sleep is overrated."

We didn't end up staring at him for hours, or at least I didn't. The next time I woke up, Emma and Vegas were gone, but as soon as I started to get up, the door opened and she came back in.

"We had another successful trip, so I think this potty-training thing is going to be a breeze." The room was filled with light and I grabbed my phone to see what time it was. Too early. I groaned, but I didn't think I could get back to sleep. There was an adorable puppy to love on.

"You want breakfast?" Emma asked, putting Vegas down and letting him romp around.

"Not yet. My stomach isn't awake. *I'm* not awake." I covered myself with the blanket. In spite of the strange sleeping arrangement and the fact that I'd been woken up by Vegas, I had slept fine. I could always nap later.

"Hey pretty boy, aren't you handsome?" Vegas danced and made snuffling noises of agreement.

"We should get him a bowtie," I said, as Emma came back from the bathroom.

"I need a shower," she said, running her hands through her tangled curls. I would never look that good in the morning. I had the feeling I was a complete disaster, but it wasn't anything Emma hadn't seen before.

"You can go first. I'll stay with Vegas and make sure he behaves himself," I said. Vegas dashed for one of his toys. I was going to teach this puppy to fetch, even if it took weeks.

"Cool. I'll start breakfast when I get out. Do you want to take him on a longer walk today? Start training him with a leash?" That seemed like a lot to put on him since we'd just gotten him home, but he did need his puppy exercise.

"Yeah, maybe we can carry him if he can't handle it." He was still small enough to hold like a baby.

"Sounds good."

∽

WE SPENT the rest of the lazy Sunday chasing Vegas around and making sure he didn't chew or pee on anything. It was a lot of work and we were both worn out.

"I think we should leave him out here tonight," Emma said, but I was completely on board with sleeping on the floor with him again.

"Just for a few more days? Until he adjusts," I said, and Emma sighed.

"I know I shouldn't agree to this, but I'm going to agree to it just for tonight. After that, we have to teach him independence. He'll be okay, I promise." I was pretty sure that Vegas might be okay, but I'd be so worried about him, I'd spend the whole night going out to check on him. Guess it was going to be an adjustment for both of us.

"What are we going to do tomorrow?" I said.

"Well, I only have class for a few hours, so we'll put him in the pen and hope he sleeps. I was looking into doggie daycare, so that's also an option. It's not going to be cheap, but I don't want him to be alone here all day. This is why I wanted to plan more beforehand, Callyn." She cracked her knuckles three times in succession, and I put my hand on her shoulder.

"It will be okay. We'll figure it out. I'll do some research." At least I could take that off her plate of worries.

She waved my hand off. "I'm sorry, I'm just stressed about school and everything. Lots of change." She gave me a tight smile and I pulled her into my arms. I realized I hadn't hugged her in a while and I needed to fix that immediately. Emma sighed and fell into me. Her hugs were always perfect. She pulled back too soon, but only because we heard whining at our feet.

"Sweet boy, we love you too." Emma picked him up and we squished him between us. Like our little furry son.

"Precious baby," I said, kissing his head. I looked up to find Emma looking at me in a way that made my blood feel hot in my veins.

"I know I seem like I'm stressed, but I just want the best for him, you know? I don't want to be a bad dog owner." She put Vegas down and I reached out to stroke her face to reassure her, but then stopped myself. Why would I do that? Stroking your best friend's face was weird, in any context.

"You won't be," I said, settling for squeezing her shoulder again. "You're going to be the best dog mom."

"I'm not sure about that, but I'm going to try. I mean, I have the additional pressure, what with going to be a vet tech and everything. I feel like I should look everything up in my books about puppies that I can find, but I feel like that's googling your medical symptoms and I probably shouldn't." I laughed.

"Yeah, maybe stay away from the chapters about canine cancer?" Emma shuddered.

"We should probably take him out again," I said. We were getting quite a workout going up and down the stairs with him. Unexpected benefit.

"Vegas, no!" she cried and dove to pull something out of his mouth.

"Where did he get this?" she asked, holding up a mangled toothpaste cap.

"The trash?" We dashed to the bathroom to find that, somehow, Vegas had overturned the trash and had ripped through it, not to mention completely shredding the toilet paper from the holder.

"I'll take him out if you clean up?" I said.

"I'll get the broom."

∼

I WOKE up before the sun the next morning (or was it still night?) to find Emma sleeping with her arm wrapped around Vegas, who was completely sacked out between us. Gently, I got up to pee and came back, but I couldn't go back to sleep again.

In the weak light, I watched Emma sleep. My best friend and fake wife and fellow dog parent. Things between us had changed so fast and I hadn't had a chance to even think about it.

She hadn't kissed me on the cheek again, so I guess that was a one-time impulse. Not that I wanted her to do it again; that was absurd. I didn't want to kiss Emma. She was my best friend.

Just because we were both queer didn't mean we had to be together or have feelings other than friendship for one another. I loved her, but not in a romantic way.

Annoyed at myself, I shut my eyes and relaxed my body, starting with my toes and working upward in an attempt to lull myself back to sleep. It took a while. My brain was busy thinking about Emma and Vegas and all kinds of strange things that I didn't want to be thinking about. Shouldn't be thinking about.

I wasn't. I wasn't thinking about anything. Just sleep.

Chapter Seven

"Guess what!" I yelled, as I walked in the door the following Thursday. I'd just gotten an extremely exciting phone call and I was so excited I was shaking.

"What?" Emma asked, looking up from wiping the floor. Probably another one of Vegas's accidents. He had his first day of doggie daycare next week, and we'd also signed him up for obedience classes at the same doggie daycare.

"I got the job!" Emma dropped the roll of paper towels and bottle of cleaner and stood up.

"Seriously?"

"Yeah, I did!" She squealed and ran over to me, sweeping me up in a lung-crushing hug. Vegas jumped up and down at our feet, begging to know what his moms were carrying on about.

"We have to celebrate. I'd say we should go out, but he's been here alone all day. Order in? Someplace fancy, definitely. Want to get the fancy pasta?" There was a place near our apartment that sold pasta with truffles on it that was incredible, but was also over fifty bucks a serving. I had had it once before, since only a very special occasion called for pasta that was that expensive.

"Yes, I need truffles. Do you need truffles, Vegas?" I picked him up and he went bananas licking my face.

"Thank you for washing my face, buddy. I needed that. Oh, yes, you're a good boy."

I set him down and Emma ordered the expensive pasta and I went to the fridge to grab a bottle of champagne. We'd replenished our stock recently.

"I'm so happy for you," Emma said, putting her hands on my shoulders from behind and leaning into me. I leaned slightly back against her as I popped the cork from the bottle.

"I'm so relieved. I'm going to be making more money, so that's good, and I really like my new boss. I mean, I like her now. I might not like her in a few weeks, but I'll burn that bridge when I get there."

"No bridge burning," she said, squeezing my shoulders and then moving away as I poured the bubbling champagne into two glasses. I missed the contact with her body, but I shoved that feeling away and turned to hand her a glass.

"To us, to new jobs and new careers and to Vegas, the cutest dog in the history of the world," I said.

"Agreed," she said, and we tapped our glasses together before sipping.

"Do you have more followers now that you started posting Vegas pictures? Because I do," I said, holding up my phone. My social following had been steadily climbing and I'd been getting more and more comments. Not that I cared about that because I didn't post that much, but it was still nice to see that other people thought my dog was as cute as I knew he was.

"Yeah, and I haven't touched the group chat because everyone has just been begging for more pictures. I think

Lara is mad." I set my glass down and pulled out one of the stools to lean on.

"Oh, she's definitely mad. I'm going to be glad when this wedding is over. What are we going to do with Vegas during the bachelorette party, part two?" I had never had to plan my life so much. Neither of us liked to leave him alone for too long, since it seemed mean.

"We can hire someone to look in on him. I actually have a friend at school whose parents are vets and she grew up training show dogs." Her phone dinged with a notification that our expensive pasta was on the way.

"Seriously? What kind of dogs?"

"All kinds, I think. She was even at Westminster a few times." Well, she certainly sounded qualified to watch our baby, but I also asked for her social handles just so I could do my own little background check. I was still working on that when the pasta got there.

"Now remember, we can't let him have any. It would make him sick," Emma said, as if I was going to secretly pass Vegas bits of pasta from my plate.

"I know, Em, I'm not going to give him any." She put the bags on the counter and I got out the plates.

"Don't think I haven't seen you passing him people food behind my back. You're like a little kid who doesn't want to eat their broccoli." I narrowed my eyes.

"That's ridiculous. I love broccoli." It was true. The best way to have broccoli was to roast it in the oven with olive oil, salt, pepper, and garlic. My mouth was watering just thinking about it.

Emma still seemed skeptical as we sat down to eat. Vegas whined at our feet and Emma got up and threw some of his toys in a corner to distract him.

"We need to teach him that he can't beg. I don't want him being the bad boy in daycare," she said.

"He's going to be the best boy and get gold stars," I said, defending him.

Emma tried to hide a smile as she shook her head.

"You're going to spoil him rotten."

"He deserves it."

Emma made a frustrated noise.

"You're hopeless."

"You love me," I said, poking her shoulder with my fork.

"Yes, I do," she said and the way she said it made me freeze for a second. I looked in her eyes and there was so much there that made my heart squeeze in my chest. My eyes wanted to fill with tears. I was completely overloaded with emotions and I had to look away before I answered her.

"I love you, too," I said, staring into my plate of pasta. Suddenly I wasn't so hungry.

∼

I WAS a nervous wreck leaving Vegas with the dog sitter on Saturday, but we had to go to Lara's bachelorette party, part two, or else she would disown us as friends and I didn't want to lose Lara. When she wasn't stressed the fuck out about her wedding, she was an awesome friend to have around and always made me laugh.

The dog sitter, Reece, was young, but Vegas raced right up to her and started doing his little happy dance and yipping, so I figured that was a pretty good endorsement.

"I can send you pictures and updates anytime. Don't worry, we're going to have fun, aren't we, precious?" Vegas licked her face and then started snuffling in her hands.

"Do you mind if I give him some treats? I make them myself for my dogs and they love them." Emma and I agreed, like good moms, and chatted a little more with Reece before heading out to catch a car to the tearoom where the first part of the party was happening. I'd decided to go fancy today, and even wore a little fascinator that I'd found online.

"Where else can I wear this?" I'd asked Emma when I bought it.

"I have no idea, but I think it would look cute on you." She'd declined my offer to buy her one, but she was all dolled up in wide-leg black pants and a gauzy white top that I would never dare wear because I would inevitably spill something on it. My mom had never allowed me to wear anything white and I'd carried that rule into adulthood. My dress looked vintage, but it was new and had a white and green toile print on it and a skirt that swirled when I moved. I loved twirling, but I had to make sure I didn't twirl too much and show the world my cash and prizes.

"You look really great today," Emma said, reaching up to adjust my green fascinator to the perfect jaunty angle.

"Thanks, so do you. I've never felt this fancy in my life. I'm totally ready to meet the queen. I practiced my curtsy this time." I still wobbled, but I think it was passable.

We arrived at the teahouse, which was attached to a hotel so fancy I didn't want to breathe near it.

"Are you sure we're allowed to be here?" I asked as we walked to the front desk and were directed to the tearoom.

"Yes, we were invited. Relax. Act like you belong here." I didn't know about that. I was going to have to really fake it. I tilted my chin up and focused my eyes right ahead and tried to walk like an heiress with no discernable talent.

"I got this," I said under my breath. Emma reached back and squeezed my hand.

"You do."

We reached the back corner of the restaurant where our group was seated and almost everyone was there. I hugged Lara's sisters, Lilly, Lila, and Lindsay (what were their parents thinking?), and said hello to a few of Lara's other family that I hadn't met before. Some aunts, a few cousins, and then there were several people from her work. Let's just say it was a more subdued crowd than the Vegas group and there probably wouldn't be any drunken marriages.

I still had a little bit of guilt about that, but so far everyone was so focused on their own lives and Lara's wedding and our cute puppy that no one had asked. Yet. Hopefully the tea wasn't spiked and I started sharing secrets, as I was wont to do when I was intoxicated.

Lilly rose from her seat with difficulty (since she was eight months pregnant) and tapped her spoon against her teacup to get everyone to be silent. "To Lara, my youngest sister, on your big day. We are so happy for you and Asa and we can't wait to see what life has in store for you. To Lara!" We all daintily raised our teacups and laughed as we clinked them together. There were finger sandwiches with things like watercress in them and little cookies that were as light as air and tiny cakes and scones with clotted cream and I decided that high tea was the shit.

"We are definitely coming here again," I said to Emma, as I slathered cream and jam on my third scone.

"We should. It's beautiful here." I hadn't looked around much, but it really was. Deep red wallpaper and chandeliers and lots of silver and the waiters all wore white gloves.

"How's the puppy?" Sammi asked. "He's so freaking cute and I'm so jealous."

Nova sighed. "You know we can't have a dog at our place, babe."

"I know," Sammi said, as she frowned.

"You can come over and see him anytime," I said. "All of you can."

"Score," Sammi said.

"After my honeymoon, definitely," Lara said.

"What's Asa doing today?" Emma asked. I'd thought that

Asa and Lara would want to have their parties together, but they'd had them separate. I loved Asa. They were so perfect for Lara and the two of them together was yet another reminder that love was real and some people were lucky enough to find it.

"They're off with their buddies doing one of those escape rooms and then going on a brewery tour." Lara made a face. "They've been bugging me to do that for a year, and I'm hoping they get it out of their system because there's no way I'm doing that." I didn't think it sounded like a bad time, but I knew how much Lara hated beer. I also would have loved to do the escape room, but tea was fine. We had board games next at a bar, so at least some alcohol would be involved eventually. Definitely not as much as we had in Vegas, I hoped. I didn't think I'd ever drink like that again.

Lara launched into all the issues they were running into for the wedding and it was boring as fuck after hearing about the same problems with the napkins and the caterer and the flowers and everything, but it would be over soon and she would go back to her regular laughing self. Hopefully.

Willa hadn't been able to come today, and I was definitely missing her. She had a last-minute family funeral for a distant relative she'd never met, but her parents had told her it was her duty to go, so she wasn't here.

We all sipped tea and ate sweets and it was nice to have something so casual, but I did have to pee a lot, which wasn't fun.

Emma's hand brushed my leg and I looked up to find her staring at me.

"What?" I asked, setting my teacup down and hoping I wasn't committing some sort of faux pas in this pristine establishment. I'd had my pinky out the whole time. You were supposed to do that, right? Should have looked it up ahead of time.

"You look really pretty today, Cal," she said, and I had that feeling in my chest again. Like someone was blowing my heart up like a balloon until it was too large for my chest and was pressing on my ribs and other organs.

"Thank you," I said in a choked voice. Why was this compliment completely turning me inside out? I'd never been really good with them, but when Emma said things like that, it was something else.

"You're welcome," she said, brushing my leg again. I flinched and my teacup clattered against the plate.

"Sorry," I said, to no one in particular.

∼

I (MOSTLY) GOT my shit together by the time we headed to the bar for board and card games. We weren't actually in the bar; they put us in a function room in the back, away from the regular customers.

The place was an old pub, and I swear you could smell the scent of a thousand spilled beers wafting up from the uneven wooden floor.

It was clean, but had just a little bit of a grungy and shabby edge to make it a haven for millennial hipsters.

The room had its own bar and bartender who (of course) was wearing a kilt and had Dropkick Murphy's playing. Lilly waddled over and had him immediately change it to something different and I was a little disappointed. The bartender, who had a conglomeration of tattoos, crossed his arms and narrowed his eyes.

"We should tip him really well for putting up with us," I said to Emma, as we took a seat at a table with Nova and Sammi.

"I swear, if we play Monopoly, I'm leaving," Nova said, making a face at the box.

"That would take way too long and I get a little too competitive when fake money is involved," I said.

"Callyn, you get competitive with any kind of game. Do you want to talk about the Scrabble Incident?" Emma said, raising her eyebrows.

"No, I would not," I said, staring at the stack of board games.

Lilly got up and announced that we were going to play each game for 20 minutes or less and then switch, so that we all got to play with each other. The three people with the highest scores would win prizes.

"When do we get to have drinks?" Sammi whispered to us.

"Probably after the first round," I said. I glanced at the bartender who was messing with his phone in boredom.

The four of us chose Go Fish since it was easy and we didn't have to think too much.

"Now, if we made this a drinking game, then that would be a party," I said, arranging my cards in my hand. I liked to fan them out perfectly.

"I don't think that will go over well," Emma said, staring at her own cards. She was concentrating and it was really cute. She wasn't as competitive as I was, but she was clever and she was sneaky. I never underestimated her when it came to games, or to anything, really.

"You're going down," she said casually, not looking up at me.

"Excuse me?" I said, looking at Nova and Sammi to see if they'd heard her.

"You're going down, Callyn," she said, smirking and then asking, "do you have any sevens?"

"Go fucking fish," I said through gritted teeth. "It's on."

She won the first game.

∼

I WON the second when we played Lara and Lilly at Sorry. Neither of us won the third game, Operation. In between games, we stuffed our faces with more food and I sucked down a rum and Coke.

We were going a total of five rounds and I was determined to win.

Emma had a gleam in her eyes that was so adorable that I couldn't help but smile. She was just so fucking cute sometimes I couldn't deal with it.

"You're not going to intimidate me by staring at me, Callyn," she said, when we were on our fourth game (Exploding Kittens). I hadn't realized I had been staring at her, but then I looked at my cards in my hand and realized I had. I needed to concentrate if I was going to beat her.

"I don't need to intimidate you. I'm above such things," I said. We were with two of Lara's coworkers and they'd been pretty quiet. It was pretty awkward, but we were making the best of it.

"Yeah, sure. I'm still going to crush you."

"Nope," I said.

She won the fourth game.

"If you don't win this next one, I have some bad news for you," she said in a sing-song voice. She'd had a few drinks and I was enjoying being with tipsy Emma. Alcohol made her more affectionate and silly. She kept touching my hair and leaning on my shoulder and making little goofy noises.

"You're on your way to being a drunky skunky, Em," I said, brushing her hair out of her face. I didn't know if she was even going to get through the fifth game, but that didn't mean I wasn't going to try and crush her while we played Candyland with two of Lara's great aunts. They were already a few drinks in and a total riot. I couldn't wait to see them at the wedding.

"King me!" one of them said, as she moved her piece on the board.

"That's checkers," the other aunt said. I could not for the life of me remember their names. I'd met too many people today and I was the worst with names. I should have requested that Lara have everyone wear nametags.

"This game would be so much better if it had actual candy involved," I said, picking a card. "Score." I landed on a shortcut and got to move even closer to the Candy Castle.

"Now I want candy," Emma said, pulling a card. "Boo." She landed on the square that meant she lost a turn. I was closer than she was, but one of the great aunts was the first one to reach the Candy Castle. She did a little dance in her chair and the other one pouted.

"This means you have to get me a cupcake." They both got up and left us there, not caring who came in second and third. I picked up another card because I was determined to win.

"Yes!" I got the right color card and made it all the way to the Candy Castle.

"I win," I said, poking Emma. She rested both arms on the table and leaned on them.

"Good for you, Callyn," she said. She didn't seem to care. "Can we take a nap now?" Sometimes when Emma drank she got super sleepy and cuddly. Guess this was one of those times.

"I know, Em. We'll go soon." This whole day was designed to end before dinner so we wouldn't be out too late. Given how tired Emma was, I was grateful.

Lilly stood in the front of the room and called everyone to attention.

"Okay, the first winner is . . . Gail!" That was one of the

great aunts. She cheered and dashed up to the front to grab the gift basket from Lilly. One of Lara's work friends got second. And third . . . "Callyn!"

I beamed at Emma and accepted my gift basket that was full of natural bath products. Oh, I was going to take over the tub with these bath bombs. Maybe I'd let Emma have a few as a consolation prize.

A few people decided to head out, and I wanted to get Emma home, and I also wanted to make sure that Vegas was okay. Reece had been sending us pictures of Vegas sleeping and even a video of him chasing a toy, but I still wanted to make sure that he hadn't missed us too much.

"Let's go home, Em," I said. She'd perked up a little bit when I got her a soda and a glass of water, but she was still a little sleepy.

We hugged Lara and said that we'd see her next weekend for brunch. She demanded more puppy pictures in the group chat, and I agreed that I would share more.

I got Emma and the gift basket into a car since I didn't want to haul the thing on a crowded train and get a bunch of looks.

"Hey, how was it?" Reece said when we walked in the door. Vegas had been asleep on the floor, but he woke right up and started barking and running in circles around us.

"Someone had a few too many drinks, I think," I said, pointing to Emma. She yawned.

"Naptime for you, young lady," I said, pushing her toward her bedroom. She shuffled off, giving Reece a wave.

"Thanks so much. I hope he wasn't any trouble," I said, picking Vegas up where he proceeded to bathe my entire face with his stinky puppy tongue. Cute and gross.

"No, he was great. He's still really young, but he's got a great personality. Really eager to please. I think you're going to have good luck training him." I counted how long Reece had been here and then sent her the amount we'd agreed upon.

"Thanks so much." I put Vegas down and he ran to get one of his toys.

"Sure, let me know if you need me to watch him again. I'd love to." I walked Reece out and then closed the door. Vegas followed me as I walked into Emma's room to find her flopped on the bed with her eyes open.

"Hey, you're supposed to be sleeping," I said, pushing her over so I could lie next to her.

"I'm not tired. Too much thinking." I turned onto my side to watch her. The late afternoon sunlight streamed in through the big window to our left and lit her up like an angel.

"What are you thinking about?" I asked.

She sighed.

"A lot of things, Callyn. A lot of things."

"Do you want to tell me some of the things so that maybe we can both think about them and then you won't have to be the only one?" She did so much for me, I wanted to try and help carry some of the weight I knew was so heavy for her. It couldn't have been easy to take me in like this and have to worry about all the bills and going to school and pleasing her parents.

"No, it's okay," she said, looking at me. "I've got this."

"You don't always have to got this. Have this. Whatever. You don't have to carry it all, Em. I can carry shit, too. I know I'm not great at it, but I want to make your life easier, not harder." I had so much guilt for being a mess most of the time. I couldn't count the times I'd gotten all tied up in knots and Emma had come and picked everything apart and fixed it for me. I didn't have to ask; she just did it. Sometimes I wish she wouldn't because then I carried the weight of having her solve my problems for me instead of me bumbling through and maybe figuring it out. I knew I needed to set some better boundaries, but we'd just been working this way our whole lives and I wasn't sure what to say to her so that we could change it and not upset her.

"I know, I know. But this is something I can carry on my own. Promise." I wanted to make her swear, but that seemed childish, so I didn't. Emma closed her eyes and rested her head back on her pillow.

"I think I will take a nap."

Vegas dashed into the room and started barking at both of us and putting his paws up on the bed. He couldn't jump up yet, so we had to pick him up if we wanted him on the bed with us. Emma was still trying to say that we shouldn't let him sleep on our beds, but then she would let him up every single time.

"Come here, baby. It's not fair that we're up here." I picked him up and put him between us. He licked Emma's face all over and she laughed. Vegas gave me the same treatment and then sighed the cutest little puppy sigh, put his head on his paws and closed his eyes.

"I wish I could go to sleep that easily," I said. "Look at me, I'm jealous of a puppy."

"Me too," Emma said, yawning.

"Do you need anything? I'll bring you some water. You should start hydrating." I was going to take care of her today. She was always taking care of me. Time to do start making things even. I left her with Vegas and went to grab water with the good ice and some ibuprofen and a little plate of snacks in case she got hungry when she woke up.

"You didn't need to do that," she said, when I came back and set everything on her nightstand.

"I'll get you anything you want, within reason," I said, and she smiled sleepily and curled her body around Vegas, like she was protecting him.

"Anything?" she asked.

"Within reason," I repeated.

"Well that's no fun," she said around a yawn. I started to back out of the room.

"Sweet dreams, Em," I said, before I closed the door.

Chapter Eight

"He's going to be fine," Emma said, as I clutched Vegas's leash in my hands. "He's going to be a good boy and have fun and make friends and then we'll see him at the end of the day. You don't want him all alone at home, do you?" I knew she was right, but I was having a hard time.

We'd toured the doggie daycare and I knew it was the right place to take Vegas and he'd have a great time, but actually leaving him here was a whole other story.

I had one more week at my hotel job before I started at the co-working space, and I didn't know how I was going to get through the day. I'd signed up for text and video updates of what Vegas was up to, but I still wanted to pop over at lunch and see him, which they had said was fine.

"You don't want to be late," Emma said gently.

I looked down at our baby and swallowed tears.

"Okay," I said. We hadn't even had him for a month, but he was such a huge part of our lives, and our lives together. Me and Emma and Vegas makes three.

Emma held the door for me and I walked in with Vegas

to the reception area. The receptionist greeted us warmly and came over to take Vegas's leash.

"Be a good boy," I said, squatting down to rub his ears and kiss his head. Emma joined me and I watched as the receptionist took him back to the playroom.

"He'll be okay," Emma said, squeezing my shoulders.

"I know he will. I'm just being dramatic, as usual." I wiped a few tears and hoped no one else saw me crying. A few other people had come in with their dogs and were dropping them off like it was no big deal. Well, their dogs weren't Vegas.

"Come on," Emma said, pulling me away.

"I don't want to go to work," I said, sniffing. "I hate that I'm making such a big deal of this, what the hell?" I wiped some more tears and Emma gave me a hug.

"He'll be fine and you're on your last week, right? You're going to go to your new job and it's going to be great and you're going to get used to this and Vegas will blossom." She probably should have told me just to snap out of it, but she didn't because that wouldn't have worked for me.

I took a deep breath and closed my eyes for a second.

"Okay," I said. I had my emotions under control. Vegas would be fine. My anxieties about him were unfounded and once this day was over, I'd see that it would be okay and then tomorrow would be a little easier.

"You good?" she asked, and I nodded.

"Yeah, I'm good." I rolled my shoulders back and cleared my throat and I was ready to face the day of work.

"Okay, I'm going to get to the library before class. You can call or text me if you need to." She gave me another quick hug before she headed off in the opposite direction. I had to take the train to work. I looked once more up at the building and considered blowing off work and going in to grab Vegas, but then I forced my feet to start walking in the direction of the closest station.

Time to focus on work and not think about how much I already missed my puppy.

∽

"HEY, I HAVE A QUESTION FOR YOU," I said to Jessika, the coworker who was also in law school. She'd been so busy that I hadn't had a chance to talk to her yet, but I caught her in the break room having a yogurt.

"Go for it," she said, licking her spoon. I sat down with my microwave pasta meal that had been a last resort lunch when I was packing my bag this morning. I got discounted hotel food, but I didn't need to spend extra money on that right now.

"So, say I have this friend who got married in Vegas and then wanted to get that marriage annulled six months later. How would my friend go about doing that?" Jessika set her yogurt down and put both hands on the table between us.

"Hold up, are you telling me that you got married in Vegas?"

"No, a friend. Wasn't me." I didn't want to get into it. I wished I was a better liar. I should have practiced this better.

Jessika tilted her head to the side and crossed her arms. Her dark eyes were skeptical.

"Callyn. Come on. We both know you're a terrible liar. So, what did you do?"

I opened my mouth to deny it again, but that wasn't going to get me anywhere. Maybe if I told her the truth she'd be more inclined to help me out. Emma had said she was going to take care of things, but I also didn't know if maybe there was a time limit, and if we stayed married and didn't get it taken care of right away, that it would bite us in the ass later.

The whole story came spilling out of my mouth. Maybe it was easier to talk to Jessika because she wasn't as close as everyone else. I also knew she was a levelheaded person and would let me know the truth without any bullshit. I kind of needed that right now.

"Well. You are in a situation, aren't you?" She rested both arms on the table and leaned forward.

"Pretty much. I mean, I went along with it because it made sense at the time, and being married to her is great. I mean, it's pretty much the same as not being married. My health insurance is better and I might get a decent tax return, but none of that is really being married. It's just financials stuff. We're not in love or anything."

Jessika had her lips pressed so hard together that I knew she had something to say.

"What?" I said.

"There are so many things I want to say right now, but I don't think you're ready to hear them. I'll do some research for you, totally, and let you know what I find. Other than that, I'd say to just keep doing what you're doing and to pay attention."

I picked up my fork to eat my now-cooling pasta. I was starving and this was better than nothing.

"Pay attention to what?" I asked.

"Just . . . pay attention," she said, tossing her empty yogurt cup in the recycling and then washing her spoon.

"Think about it," she said, patting my shoulder before exiting the kitchen and leaving me to my thoughts. What did she mean? I pondered while munching my pasta until someone came to use the microwave to reheat some sort of fish thing and I had to leave or gag on the rest of my lunch. Why were people like that?

I SPENT the rest of my day alternately worrying about Vegas and thinking about what Jessika had said. Did she mean pay attention to Emma? Pay attention to the legal ramifications? Both? I wanted to ask Emma to help me figure it out, but I didn't want her to know I'd told someone what we'd done. So I was stuck relying on my own brain to figure it out.

I stared at the time clock and punched out as soon as I could to race to the train so I could get to Vegas. I was meeting Emma so we could take him home together.

I beat her to the doggie daycare, but I waited until she came in through the door, her hair blowing all around her with the wind, before going inside.

"Sorry, sorry, I got stuck in study group. Let's go get him," she said, and I wanted to grab her hand again. I'd had that urge more and more lately and I had no idea what it meant.

The receptionist brought Vegas out to us and I cried again when I saw him.

"Were you a good boy today? Were you?"

"He was great," the receptionist said, handing us a printout. We'd also gotten updates on the app about his behavior, but this was nice to see his first day report card.

"Come on sweetheart, let's go home," I said, trying to lead the wiggly puppy through the door while Emma held it. I honestly wanted to pick him up and cuddle him the whole way, but he was off and running, pulling on the leash and then focusing on a spot on the sidewalk and refusing to move on until we coaxed him.

"I can't wait until he's really trained," I said. It took so long to get him home that Emma did end up picking him up for the last little bit.

"Soon," she said. "Soon he will be. We're going to have

to be diligent about it, though. Constant reinforcement and all that." I'd done a little bit of research and I was all in on making sure that Vegas was a well-trained boy. It was bad dog parenting to not train your dog. Plus, puppies needed boundaries, just like children.

"How was your day?" I asked, after we walked through the door. She seemed tired and I wondered if she was sleeping well.

"Long," she said, putting her bag down with a thump. "Would you mind making dinner tonight?" I almost fell over. Emma didn't ask me to cook. I couldn't remember any time she had asked me that.

"Yeah, of course," I said, scrambling to the fridge to figure out what I could throw together that would be decent and that I wouldn't mess up.

Pasta. I could do pasta. I found a box and a bottle of sauce and some defrosted chicken. I could do that. Probably.

"Is spaghetti chicken okay?" I asked her. Emma was on the couch cuddling with Vegas.

"Yeah, sounds good." I found some frozen asparagus I thought would make a good side dish. It wasn't up to Emma's culinary standards, but I was going to do my best not to fuck it up too badly.

~

EMMA JOINED me in the kitchen fifteen minutes later as I drained the pasta and mixed it in with the chicken and sauce. I'd made a mess with the sauce splattering everywhere, but I hadn't burned the chicken or the sauce, and everything was cooked through, so I thought I had done a good job.

Emma wearily got out the plates and used tongs to place the pasta on our plates, topping it with the chicken, and then putting the asparagus on the side of her plate. She grabbed a separate plate for my asparagus. I didn't like my foods touching, especially if there was a sauce component.

"Thank you," I said, when she handed me my plate.

"Do you want to eat on the couch? I feel like watching something." Emma didn't usually allow that, so I was really on high alert.

"Are you feeling okay?" I asked, as we grabbed paper towels and drinks and brought everything to the couch.

"Yeah, just tired. I don't know."

"Maybe you're coming down with something?" I asked, reaching out to feel her forehead. She flinched away from my touch.

"What the hell, Em?" She waved me off and picked up her plate.

"Sorry. I'm just . . . Sorry." What was going on? I started to ask her, but she looked straight ahead and turned on the TV.

Emma and I had had our fights before as all best friends had. There had been times when we hadn't spoken, but those were few and far between.

"Will you please talk to me? I can't handle it when you shut me out," I said. She closed her eyes and I thought she was going to cry.

"I'm sorry. I just need some space right now to think about a lot of things, okay? I just . . . I need some space." I wasn't going to lie, that hurt.

"Space from me?" I asked, my stomach knotting up with anxiety. Emma still wouldn't look at me.

"I just need some space," she said again, not answering my question, which was an answer in itself. I looked away from her and tried not to cry. I pulled Vegas onto my lap and let him gnaw on my fingers, even though it hurt like hell.

When had things gone so sideways? Everything had been fine this morning. Maybe she was getting tired of living with me. Maybe I was stressing her out. Maybe she was regretting the puppy. Maybe it was all of those things.

I shouldn't have moved in here. I should have found some other crappy roommates and left her alone. There was that saying that you didn't truly know someone until you lived with them. We'd been friends for so long, but had never lived together. I guess Emma didn't like what she found when I moved in.

My head spun with all sorts of terrible things and I started to feel sick. I couldn't imagine my life without Emma. She was everything to me.

I kept my mouth shut and pretended to watch the show and that I was fine and I was completely calm. Emma asking for space was a reasonable request and I could do that. It wasn't Emma's fault that I immediately thought the worst when anything happened.

Using the breathing exercises I'd learned from my meditation app, I tried to calm myself and not get all twisted up in imagining scenarios that would never come to pass. Vegas seemed to sense my agitation and started licking my arm, as if to comfort me. He was such a precious boy.

Emma and I sat in silence for a long time and I was barely keeping a lid on my panic. At last I grabbed our plates and went to the kitchen to put them in the dishwasher and then get Vegas some fresh water. He went to town, slopping and slurping water everywhere.

"We're going to need to put a towel under your bowl, you goober," I said, patting his head.

Emma went to the bathroom while I was petting Vegas and didn't come back. I went and knocked on the door.

"Em, are you okay? I know you wanted space, but I can't

take this anymore." My voice broke and the door opened. Emma had been crying.

"I'm sorry," she said, sobbing and throwing herself at me. I opened my arms to catch her and she collapsed.

"What's wrong? My god, Em." I rubbed her back and was starting to get really concerned that something terrible had happened that she didn't want to tell me.

She lifted her face from my shoulder and looked into my eyes. Her eyelashes were stuck together by tears. I wiped her cheeks with both thumbs.

"Talk to me," I said, as I cradled her face in my hands. Seeing her cry was making me want to cry as well, and I was fighting the urge.

"I can't," she finally said in a choked voice. She closed her eyes and leaned forward a fraction. Our noses were almost touching.

"I can't talk to you," she said, and I heard Jessika's words in my head again, *pay attention*.

"What can you do?" I asked, and every cell in my body was waiting for the answer. Something was happening, I could feel it in the charged air between us. Everything was about to change, but it was still a shock when Emma pressed her lips to mine for a fraction of a breath before she pulled back. Or, at least she tried to pull back, because I was still holding onto her face. I wouldn't let her go. Without thinking of even one single consequence, I did what I do best: I gave in to my first impulse and this time I kissed her. It was a little bit longer than her micro-peck, but it still probably didn't qualify as an actual kiss. So I tried again. This time I took a step closer and inhaled through my nose as I adjusted to the kiss. Emma still seemed to be in shock, so I rubbed my thumbs on her cheeks to relax her.

I had no idea what came over me but, suddenly, kissing

Emma seemed like the most important thing in the entire world.

I pulled back a bit, only to touch her lips again. I swear she tasted like an orange. My legs wobbled and I was just starting to think I'd done the wrong thing when she opened her mouth and sighed, as if in relief. Once that happened, all hell broke loose.

Chapter Nine

IT WASN'T JUST A KISS. It was a seduction, it was a devouring, it was a surrender. It was everything at once and I couldn't breathe and I didn't want it to stop. My hands moved from Emma's face to grip her shoulders, as if to have something to hold onto to ground me. Otherwise I might have either floated away or melted into the floor.

Her mouth was warm and vicious. She kissed me as if I was her salvation. I felt the same way as our lips slowly caressed each other. Not hurrying. Not rushing. Emma kissed me hard and deep. At first, there was a bit of fumbling, trying to fit our faces together so we could kiss and breathe and get everything lined up the right way, but we got there after a few moments. I nearly blacked out when she slipped her tongue between my lips. I'd never been a huge fan of making out, but this was . . . something else. Something entirely different.

Sparks exploded behind my eyelids and I reached for her tongue with mine, desperate to taste as much of her as possible. I wanted to fill my lungs with nothing but her. I didn't need air right now.

Emma tried to slow the kiss down, but now I was desperate and hungry and I'd only had a small sip of what we could have together and I wanted to drown myself in it. She made a little sound that might have been a moan but, finally, Emma pulled her mouth away.

"Cal. What are we doing?" I groggily opened my eyes. My lips were swollen and tender and it took a moment to come down from wherever I'd gone mentally during the kiss. Another planet, probably. Maybe another dimension.

I couldn't make any words come out of my mouth, but my brain had started to register that Emma and I had kissed. I kissed my best friend. Friends didn't make out with friends. At least, not usually.

"Cal?" she said.

"Uh huh," I squeaked out. "What?"

"Callyn," she said, but I was too mesmerized by the shifting colors in her eyes and the way her cheeks had gotten a little pinker, as if she'd slicked on a cheek stain.

"Huh?" I replied. Now she was the one putting both hands on my face.

"Callyn, I need you to focus. We just kissed and I think we need to discuss it," she said.

"Why?"

She made a frustrated sound and all I could think of was kissing her lips again. I needed to spend a significant portion of my day kissing Emma. I didn't even want to think about all the years I'd spent not kissing her. What a waste. Complete fucking waste of time.

Emma put both her hands on my shoulders and actually pushed me so I was a few feet away from her. My head started to clear a little and it became easier to breathe once I had some space between us.

"Callyn, this . . . I didn't mean for this to happen, holy

shit." She wrenched both hands through her hair, getting her fingers tangled.

"But it did happen and I want it to keep happening. Kiss me, please." Emma shook her head.

"No, that's a bad idea. A very bad idea."

"Bad ideas are the best ideas," I said, stepping toward her again. "Let's have bad ideas together." I didn't know what had come over me, but I was possessed by someone much more confident than I was.

"Come here, Emma Christine" I said, and kissed her gently enough that she could stop it if she wanted to. I knew her well enough to know when she wanted to do something and when she didn't. Her words said one thing, and then her body said something completely different.

"If you want me to stop, tell me," I said, pulling back.

"We should stop." I brushed my nose against hers.

"That wasn't what I asked you. If you really don't want me to kiss you again, I will never kiss you again. Just say the words. Or, if you can't say it, put one hand on my chest."

I waited for what felt like three thousand years, our noses almost touching, our eyes locked on each other. I think we both even stopped breathing.

I felt her breath wash across my face as she said, "I want you to kiss me again."

"Okay," I said, because what else was there to say? I needed to use my lips for something much better than talking.

I smiled as she leaned forward, kissing me instead, even though she'd asked me to kiss her. Things started slow and sweet again, soft brushes and light pressure. As if we were still testing this out. In a way, we were. I was standing here and kissing my best friend, who I definitely had never thought of kissing.

Right?

Emma laughed a little and I froze.

"Stop thinking," she said, and I almost fell over.

"That's my line."

"I know. I'm not really sure who I am right now, but I don't care." I kissed the tip of her nose.

"You're Emma and I'm Callyn." It was the first thing that came to mind.

"Okay," she said, as if that was a satisfactory answer and went back to kissing me.

All of my nerve endings concentrated themselves on my mouth, or at least it felt that way. Every single slide of her lips against mine set me on fire and then she got her tongue involved again and I was completely and utterly lost.

After only a few moments (or it could have been a few hours, I had no fucking idea), I realized that my legs were trembling so bad that I could barely stand. I needed to at least sit down. After only a second of thought, I broke the kiss again and said, "Come with me."

To her credit, Emma followed me into my bedroom. I shut the door, even though that would leave a whining Vegas on the other side. He would survive a little time on his own. I pressed my back to the door and watched Emma. Her chest was heaving as if she'd run up the stairs and her pupils were larger than normal. She looked a little wild and I wondered if her heart was beating as fast as mine.

I crossed the room and sat on my bed which, of course, wasn't made, but why did that matter right now?

"Come here," I said again. I almost patted the bed next to me but stopped myself at the last minute.

She was hesitating again.

"We can stop this right now if you want. We can go back out there and watch a movie and sit next to each other on the couch. Or you can come here and we can see where this is going to go." Inside I was screaming at her to pick the second option, but I would never try and talk her into something she didn't want. Never ever.

"I don't want to stop," she said, closing her eyes. I could feel her making a decision in her mind, weighing the options. Emma might take longer than me to make a decision, but once she made it, she was all in.

Her eyes snapped open and I waited for the verdict.

"I'm not going to stop," she said, and I nearly slid off the bed. "Not until you tell me to. Or I come to my senses. Whichever comes first."

I couldn't even comprehend what those words meant other than that she was going to keep kissing me. That was the most important.

Emma walked over to the bed and lay down. Her eyes were sparks of blue and green fire.

"Come here," she said. I tried to swallow, but my mouth was too dry.

We were doing this. I didn't know how far it would go, but I was ready to find out.

I took one deep breath before stretching out next to Emma on the bed.

I turned on my side, unsure of what to do. She scooted closer and tucked some of my hair out of my face.

"You're so goddamn beautiful," she said. Emma had told me I was gorgeous before. Hundreds, maybe thousands, of times. This was different. The words were the same, but they had a completely different meaning.

"So are you," I said.

Her mouth met mine and the kiss was different as well. Moving to the bed seemed to have escalated everything. This time her tongue wasn't gently caressing the inside of my mouth. No, her tongue was on a mission to decimate me.

It was working.

I reached for her and she rolled until she was on top of

me, and I moaned from her weight. It took a few tries to get our mouths aligned the right way, but we got there and then she was on the attack again. As if they had minds of their own, my hands slid down her body to cup her ass and I nearly stopped the kiss to ask her why I hadn't been touching her ass before this moment. It was the most perfect ass. Not that I'd had a lot of ass-grabbing experience, but HOLY SHIT. I squeezed and she made a little yelping noise.

"Sorry," I said, removing my hands.

"No, I was just surprised. Don't stop." Those last two words were the only words I ever wanted to hear Emma say again.

So I grabbed her ass again and squeezed and I was rewarded with her slowly pressing her hips into mine and I definitely blacked out for a second. So much was happening and my body was overloading. Emma's lips, Emma's tongue, Emma's teeth, Emma's hips, Emma's hands. She was everywhere at once and my body didn't feel like it belonged to me anymore. I belonged to *her*.

I stopped thinking and let myself completely feel everything and anything, including Emma's hand that was making its way under my shirt.

Kissing was one thing, but this kind of touch led to . . . a whole lot more. All the possibilities exploded in my brain like bright fireworks. Emma's touch was electric and I wouldn't have been surprised if I was actually glowing. My shirt rode up and my bare skin touched hers and I knew that I wanted more. More contact. More skin. I wrenched my mouth away from hers.

"Take your shirt off. Please." I added the last word because it sounded like a command and I wanted to be nice.

Emma didn't second-guess me. Nope. She yanked her shirt over her head and threw it on the floor. I'd never seen

Emma throw a shirt on the floor. Her clothes always went right into the hamper. Who was she right now?

Her bra was black and simple, but holy shit, she looked incredible. I'd seen her in a bra before, but it was hitting me that Emma had taken off her shirt because I'd asked her to, and as pretty as the bra was, I was more interested in what was under it.

I pulled at the front of her bra, right where the cups met, as if I could pull it off that way. Emma looked down at me, her cheeks flushed and her eyes feverish.

"Take this off," I said, and it almost sounded like a whine. As if I was a child begging for a piece of cake. Right now I'd rather have what was under Emma's bra than all the cake in all the world, and that was saying something because I loved cake.

Emma reached behind her and unclasped her bra, and it went sailing across the room to hang out with her shirt on the floor. Nearly every other time I'd ever seen Emma without a shirt on, I'd always looked away. I told myself it was out of respect. I rationalized it in any way I could. Now that I saw her in all her glory, I knew it was because I couldn't handle the sight of her incredible boobs. Absolutely top notch. Eleven stars. I would write reviews of them all over the internet.

"What now?" she asked, as if I was steering this ship. I guess until now I had been.

"I want to touch you," I said, but I didn't know if I could actually do it. Looking was one thing. Touching was crossing a boundary.

"Then touch me," she said, moving her hair over her shoulder. I should have put mine up before we started all this, but I couldn't have predicted this was going to happen tonight, or any other night.

I held up my hands and looked at them. They didn't feel like they belonged to me.

Emma reached for my hands and lifted them for me, keeping her eyes locked on mine. Gently, she placed a hand on top of each of her breasts so I could feel her soft-as-silk skin, interrupted only by the hardness of her nipples.

"Fuck," I breathed out. Emma sighed and threw her head back, arching herself into my hands. I grazed her nipples with my thumbs, marveling at how hard they got. I'd touched a boob or two in my time, but that had been more of a cursory touch on the way to something else. I'd never paid attention like this before.

I cupped them in my hands, feeling their weight. I probably could have messed with them for hours, but I wanted to make *her* feel good, so I focused my attention on stroking her nipples. She liked that, judging by her reaction.

I wanted to taste her. It was a struggle to let go of her nipples, but I needed my arms to prop myself up so I could get my mouth where it needed to be. Emma sensed what I was trying to do and leaned down.

Fuck. Me.

I took one nipple in my mouth and the sound she made went right between my legs, as if she had physically touched me.

I decided to try something and bit down lightly with my teeth before adding a little bit of suction.

"Fuck," she said, and I felt her legs tremble in response. She definitely liked that. I kept going, doing whatever struck my fancy before moving to treat the other nipple with the same care. She was halfway bare and panting and I still had all my work clothes on. It probably wasn't fair, but I didn't mind. I was having the time of my life pleasuring her.

"Oh, Cal," she sighed, and I knew I wanted her under me. I pushed into a sitting position and then pushed her shoulder until she lay down on the bed. Now it was my turn to straddle her and look down. She was incredible from this angle too.

Her nipples were wet and glistening from my mouth.

"Your turn," she said, panting a little.

"What?" I was too busy staring at her tits and thinking about biting them. I wanted to see my teeth marks on her skin.

"Take your shirt off, Callyn," she said, tugging at the hem of my shirt. Oh, right. I guess that was only fair. I'd have to save the biting for later.

I pulled my shirt over my head and didn't even pause before I removed the bra as well. Might as well get it all in one go.

"You like?" I asked.

"Oh, yes. I always have," she said, and now I was the one getting boob touches. I'd never really thought about this as a sexual thing, but the minute Emma's fingers caressed my nipples, I thought I was going to come.

"Holy fucking shit," I said, looking down at her in wonder.

"Good?" she asked.

"Hell yeah, do that again," I said. She flicked one with her fingers and then pinched it just a little bit.

"Yes," was the only word I could come up with. She gave each nipple the same treatment at the same time and I jerked as if I'd been struck by lightning.

"Noted," she said, under her breath. Of course Emma was cataloging all my reactions. I bet there was some sort of list she had going in her head. I just hoped she didn't actually write any of this shit down. That would be a little too weird.

"I'm going to taste you," she said, and then she did, after waiting for a second to give me the chance to stop her. So thoughtful.

I didn't stop her. I wasn't going to stop her from any of her natural instincts right now. I knew Emma well enough to know she wasn't going to, like, start nomming on my feet or something. At least I hoped not. I didn't think I had a foot fetish . . .

My mental tangent on foot fetishes was interrupted by Emma's warm mouth on my right nipple. That just shut down any kind of thought right there.

I'd never had my nipples sucked before, but Emma was doing an incredible job. She flicked them with her tongue and sucked with an incredible amount of pressure and bit them just hard enough to send a little zing of pain through me. My entire body ached with need. I was rushing toward something intense and life altering.

"Do you like that?" she asked, and I opened my eyes (I couldn't remember closing them) and looked down to find her looking up at me with uncertainty in her eyes. Guess I needed to be more vocal. I wasn't normally a quiet person, but I'd been so caught up that I guess I'd made her think something was wrong.

"I've never been this horny in my fucking life and if I don't come soon, I will probably die. And you're really, really good at that. Everything you're doing is the best thing I've ever . . . I don't even know. I can't speak, Em. I'm brain-dead from horniness."

She shook her head slowly and smiled.

"You have a way with words, Callyn."

"You have fantastic tits, Emma." That made her laugh. "Seriously, I could write fucking sonnets in iambic pentameter and I don't even know what that is, but I'd find out and do it for you. And your boobs." I looked down at them lovingly. Why wasn't I biting them again? Oh, right, because Emma was busy biting mine.

"You don't need to do that, but it's nice to hear?" I

pushed my annoying hair out of my way again and ran my hand down her chest, stopping right at the waistband of her jeans. I flicked the button open and met her eyes, silently asking if she wanted to stop me.

"Nope. You first this time." I squealed as I somehow ended up on my back with Emma on her stomach next to me. She had the button of my pants undone and the zipper pull between her fingers.

"Do it," I said, and she yanked that zipper down so fast, I thought she was going to rip it right out of my pants. In a flash, she was down by my ankles and trying to yank my pants off that way. They were a little tight, so instead of pulling them off, she just pulled me further down the bed.

"That worked out much better in my head," she said, as I lifted my hips and helped her get my pants down my legs. They got stuck on one foot and I had to shake them off.

I wish I'd worn cuter underwear today. At least I didn't have one of the pairs that I wore during my period because they were old and ugly and stained and I didn't care about them anymore.

This pair had fluffy llamas on them. Maybe they weren't the sexiest, but they were cute. They'd almost gotten pulled off with my pants, but that was the last frontier and I didn't know if I was ready for that part just yet.

"Nice," Emma said, glancing at my undies. I wondered what color hers were.

"Nothing sexier than llama panties," I said, and she laughed and slowly crawled back up toward me.

"Now take yours off. I want to know if we match." I tugged at the button of her jeans.

"We're not matching, but I'll take off my pants so you can check anyway." She started to pull them down and if I wasn't lying down, I would have fallen over.

"You're not wearing anything," I said, stating the obvious.

"I never do with these jeans," Emma said, grinning as she threw her jeans on the floor. She was completely naked next to me and I didn't know what part of her to look at first. This was quickly taking its place as the best day of my whole damn life.

"You're naked," I said.

"Yes, I am. Is that okay?"

"Oh, no, put your clothes back on," I said sarcastically. Emma rolled her eyes and blushed.

"It's been a while since I've been naked with someone," she said. "And it's different with you. I feel like you've already seen me naked, so this shouldn't be anything new."

It was true that technically I'd seen her naked, but not really.

"I couldn't look at you. It felt wrong, to stare at your best friend when she was changing for gym or whatever. So I never *really* looked." Emma's smile turned shy and I could tell this wasn't easy for her. I was still clinging to a few scraps of llama fabric.

"So, look now," she said, after taking a deep breath. "I want you to look."

I wanted to do more than look, but I settled for that right now. She was glorious. I took in everything: the softness of her belly, the roundness of her breasts, the whiteish stretch marks on her sides and thighs, the dark spots and freckles and scars. Every single inch of her was perfection. I couldn't see the cheeky little cherry tattoo on her right ass cheek, but I hoped I'd get a good view of it soon.

"You're beautiful." She was so pretty it made me want to cry.

"You make me feel beautiful, Callyn," she said.

"Can I touch you?" I asked. She was on her side and I was on mine facing her. She rolled onto her back.

"Yes."

I started with her face because that seemed like the right thing to do. I let my fingers caress her cheeks, her lips, walk up and down her nose. I'd never touched her like this before and it was a revelation.

I realized then that I had wanted to touch her like this for as long as I could remember. It was always there, in the back of my mind, but I'd pushed it so far aside, it had lurked behind the shadows, just waiting for me to be ready. I didn't know if I was ready yet, but it was happening.

She swallowed hard as I touched her throat, pausing briefly to take her pulse. It fluttered like a hundred angry butterflies. I spent some more time on her fabulous tits, giving them the attention they deserved.

Emma had had started to squirm and grip the blankets.

"Something wrong?" I asked. I was enjoying this slow torture. I wanted to go even slower, to tease her as much as I possibly could, but I was also getting impatient.

I wanted to make her come so hard she would never forget it. At least twice. I wanted to make this the best night of her life because it was already mine. Seeing her like that would probably make me come, so it would benefit both of us in the end.

"No, I just . . . I need . . ."

"I know what you need," I said. "But I'm not going to give it to you yet. I'm busy." I circled her bellybutton and moved a little lower. Her entire body trembled.

I veered down to her legs and started caressing her calves.

"You are a terrible person, Callyn Jean."

"Damn right, Emma Christine." Any retort on her part was lost as her legs twitched and scissored against the bed.

"I'm getting there, my goodness. You're more impatient than I am." I made a note of that.

"I'm sorry, I can't help it. I haven't come in so long, Callyn." Fuck me, that was both the saddest and the hottest thing she'd ever said.

"Tell me about it. Tell me about the last time you came. Did you use your hand?" I wanted to know. I needed to know every single detail.

"Yes. I used my hand with some lube. It's too much friction otherwise." Her eyes shuttered closed as I brushed my hand up and down her thigh, getting closer and closer to where she wanted me with each pass.

"What did you think about when you touched yourself?"

It took her what felt like a year to answer.

"You. I thought about you."

My hand stalled. That was the last thing I was expecting her to say. I'd expected maybe the name of a celebrity or perhaps a fetish that I didn't know about, but not that. Not *me*.

"Me?" I questioned. I needed her to say it again.

Her eyes seared into me and she took my hand and squeezed it before placing it where she wanted me.

"You," she said, pressing my hand down and letting her eyes flutter closed. "Always you."

My hand was sandwiched between hers and her . . . well. I didn't want to say vulva. That felt too clinical and weird. Junk didn't seem romantic. Mound was just strange and made me think of mountains or something.

Emma's fingers clenched and she pushed herself into my hand and moaned so loud I forgot about what to call the area and got to work touching it. I rubbed her gently, realizing too late that my hand was a little dry. I removed it and she popped her eyes open and made a sound of protest until she saw me slowly licking my hand before touching her again.

"That was hot," she said, and then her eyes jerked closed again as I stroked her up and down, moving to explore new territory. I fingered her entrance, noticing at how smooth and slightly damp she was. I hoped that was due in part to me. I wanted to make her feel good. I wanted to make her come so hard she wondered if she was going to survive it.

I also wanted to do something else and I went with it. I stuck my index finger in my mouth to make sure it was wet enough and then slid it inside her. She arched up and moaned so loud that I thought the neighbors could hear her. Hell yeah, I wanted them to hear. I wanted everyone to hear what I was doing to her.

"*Callynnnnnn*," she breathed, and it was the sweetest sound in the entire world. I didn't have much experience finger-fucking someone else but I did it a lot to myself, so I tried to flip things around and do what I liked, just on her. It took some finagling, but I finally got the hang of it and found what made her squirm and moan and beg.

"Look at me," I said, withdrawing my finger slowly. Her eyes opened and her thighs jerked as I held up my finger, wet from her, and licked it. She tasted like salt and sweetness and I swear I could taste a hint of orange on the back of my tongue.

"Fuck," she said, "how are you so sexy?" I almost laughed because I didn't think of myself as sexy. I'd tried, and I always came off as awkward or trying too hard. Things were different with Emma, though.

"Mmm, you're the sexy one, Em. Always have been, always will be." She started to protest, but it turned into a gasp when I dove between her legs and sucked her clit into my mouth. Her legs clamped on my head so hard I thought she might have crushed all the cartilage in my ears. Small price to pay.

This was also a pretty new experience for me, but I learned quickly what Emma liked. Once I got a good routine going, I added my finger, fucking her on the inside and drove her hard, feeling with my finger and my tongue when she was close and backing off before she came. Mean, but it was going to be worth it.

"You are a horrible person," she said, the third time I did it.

"No, I'm a wonderful person and you will thank me," I said, licking my lips. I was going to need a towel to wipe off my face after this.

"Please, I can't take much more." Her knuckles were white as they gripped the blankets and her legs thrashed.

"I guess I've tortured you enough. Are you ready to come?" She glared down at me.

"If you don't let me come in the next thirty seconds, I'm going to murder you." I almost burst out laughing, but she looked pretty damn serious.

"Fine, fine. Don't get your panties all twisted."

"Shut up and suck my clit." I was so shocked my mouth dropped open. I'd never heard Emma talk like that before. Granted, I'd never gone down on Emma before so maybe this was a new facet of her personality that I was just getting to witness.

"As you wish," I said, and went back to sucking her clit and flicking it with my tongue and remembering to give her labia some love as well. I fucked her hard with my fingers, curling them to hit that special spot inside her that would make her scream. I didn't count (because I was busy with other things), but just about thirty seconds later her thighs smushed my ears again and her back arched and she called out as her hips jerked with her release. It went on for a while,

Didn't Stay in Vegas

and I kept it going as long as I could until I could tell she was done. I rested my cheek on her leg and looked up at her.

"Thank you," she said.

"You're very welcome, Emma. It was my pleasure." Literally. I was hornier than I'd ever been in my entire life. I could probably come with minimal effort, but I wanted her to bask in her own orgasm before I started thinking about my own. This moment was for her.

She stroked my damp hair away from my face.

"You're a mess," she said with a warm smile.

"I'm your mess." Her chest was damp from sweat, but she was glowing, like she was lit from within. I was responsible for that. The feeling of power struck me so hard that I wanted to get up and shout from the rooftops. I wanted everyone to know that I had made Emma look and feel like that.

"That was amazing," Emma said, looking up at the ceiling. "I've never come that hard. I didn't know I *could* come that hard. Jesus, Callyn."

I buried my face between her legs again to hide my blush. I couldn't deal with this level of compliments.

"Hey, look at me," she said, tugging at my hair. I lifted my head and rested my chin on her leg.

"What?" I said.

"You were amazing. And it wasn't just what you did. It's because it was you. Come here." She lifted my chin and guided me forward. I scooted up until my face was level with hers. I wasn't sure if she'd want to kiss me, but she lifted her face until our lips touched.

"Thank you," she said again.

"You're welcome." Her smile turned wicked and a shiver went down my spine.

"Good. Now sit on my face."

THAT WAS COMPLETELY new territory for me, but fuck it, I was going to sit on my best friend's face and fuck her like there was no tomorrow.

It took a little adjusting and giggling and blushing (on my part mostly), but I got where I needed to be and thanked her for buying a guest bed with a solid headboard because it gave me something to hold onto. It was quite the view looking down between my legs to find Emma looking up at me.

"Am I suffocating you?" I asked, lifting my hips a little. I was worried about her ability to breathe right now.

"Nope," she said, and then that wicked smile returned and then I wasn't thinking about Emma being able to breathe. I wasn't thinking about anything at all. I was taken over by the all-consuming pleasure of Emma licking my most intimate place. I wanted to write songs about her mouth and its ability to completely turn me inside out. Had she been doing some sort of special exercises? Where had she learned to do all of this?

It didn't matter, and my thoughts were increasingly getting pushed out of my brain by the building intensity that was threatening to destroy me.

I wasn't even in control of my body as I thrust my hips against her mouth and made so many sounds I didn't even know I could make and I'm pretty sure I heard some muffled moans from Emma. I really hoped I wasn't killing her because then we could never do this again. That would be the worst.

I could feel the climax coming and just as I was teetering on the edge, she stopped. Terrified that I'd hurt her, I froze, which was the most difficult thing I'd ever done in my life.

"Are you okay?" I panted, looking down. I had to move my hips back so she could answer me.

"Yeah, I'm just paying you back for what you did to me." I wanted to scream. I wanted to shake her. I wanted to kiss her.

I couldn't even speak, so a bunch of sputtering noises emerged instead.

"It's only fair, Cal," she said. "Would you like me to continue?"

"Yeah," I said. At least I could form that word. It was the most important.

"Then get back up here. I'm enjoying this too much. And I can't wait to feel you come on my tongue." I couldn't wait for that either, so I got back in position and she started again from the beginning. Slow and deep and torturous. Emma fucked me hard with her tongue and her mouth and I couldn't hold out anymore and fell over the edge and into the abyss where nothing existed but what was happening in my body. I was drowning in the most intense sensations that I had ever felt. Wave after wave crashed on top of me, and I didn't think it would ever end. Emma did her part and kept up the intensity, making the climax last even longer than I thought possible.

When the last little shudders started to subside, I felt like I could fall immediately asleep and stay that way for a year. My skin tingled and sparked, and it was almost too much.

I somehow swung my leg over and collapsed on the bed next to Emma, still panting and struggling to keep my eyes open.

"You are really good at that," I said. "Did you take a class? Did you read a book? Because that was something else. Are you still alive? Are you still breathing?" I turned my head, with major effort, and she looked at me. Her face was red and glistening from me. I liked how she looked right now. Even her hair was a mess, which I'd seen only a handful of times before.

"I just trusted my instincts and did what I would want done. That was the first time I've done that, but I've been thinking about it for a lot longer. I may have watched some videos." My eyes went wide.

"Are you telling me that you watch porn?" That was something completely unexpected. I mean, I did, but I'd never told her that. There were only a few secrets I kept from Emma and that was one of them.

"Yes, why is that shocking? A lot of people watch porn," she said, a little defensive. I turned on my side.

"Hey, don't be upset. I guess I just never saw you that way. You always got weird whenever sex came up, so I thought it made you uncomfortable, and I didn't want you to be, so I stopped talking about it." I was being crushed under too many revelations tonight. It was going to take me a year to work through everything that had happened in the past few hours. Maybe even longer than that.

"I got weird when I talked about sex around *you*. There was a reason for that. Can you imagine what it was?" I wrapped some of her damp hair around my fingers.

"I'm guessing it has something to do with the fact that we're both naked in my bed and we just fucked? Holy shit, we just fucked." Reality was starting to come back to me in drips and drops now that the glow from our orgasms was starting to dim.

I just fucked my best friend. The best friend that I never, ever, EVER thought I would fuck.

Ok, maybe not NEVER, ever. I might have thought about Emma in a sexy way before. A few times. Definitely more lately, but I'd pushed those thoughts aside so forcefully that I'd hidden them from myself.

"Yeah, we just fucked. And we kissed," she said. I wasn't sure what the distinction was there, since it seemed to me like it was all part of the same package.

"And what the fuck happens now?" I jumped as she stroked my hip. We were both still completely naked and I was starting to get a little chilly from the drying sweat.

Emma closed her eyes and let out the biggest breath.

"I have no idea."

One thing was for sure: our friendship would never be the same.

Chapter Ten

I WANTED to ask her a million questions and I wanted to ask myself a million more. Instead of doing that, I said I needed to take a shower and Emma asked if she could come with me. A microscopic part of me wanted some space from her so I could think, but the majority of me was too horny for that, so I said she could.

We ended up getting dirtier instead of cleaner in the shower and she fucked me standing with her fingers while I tried to hold onto the shower bar so my legs wouldn't collapse beneath me. Then I paid her back by doing the same thing and she braced her back on the wall and lifted her leg so I could get a better angle and I decided to try going down on her again, but nearly drowned in the spray, so that was a fail, but we both laughed and I finished her with my hand anyway. Before the water got cold, we did a quick wash of all our important parts. It was seriously late and I was going to be a mess for work tomorrow, but none of that mattered. Emma wrapped me in a towel and I followed her into her room.

"You going to watch?" she asked, as she grabbed some pajamas from her drawer.

"I mean, yes? If that's okay." I'd always stopped myself from admiring her at all so, as a result, I hadn't gotten to appreciate her incredible body. Seriously, WOW.

"It's a little weird," she said, but dropped her towel anyway. She turned her back to me which gave me a great view of her ass, and that sweet little tattoo. It was generous and round and I wanted to bite it. Emma looked at me over her shoulder.

"You're looking at me like you want to eat me."

"I do. I want to eat all of you. In a non-cannibalistic way. In a sexy way." I was not that great at this. I was beginning to see why I was single so often.

"Thanks, I think?" I went back to staring at her ass as she put on a tank and then slipped on some bottoms. No undies there either.

"Why didn't I know that you don't wear underwear most of the time?" I feel like that was something I should have known.

"I don't know." She lifted one shoulder and dropped it before picking up her towel and tossing it in the hamper.

She crossed her arms and nodded at me.

"Your turn."

"I don't have clothes in here," I said.

"I don't care. You got to see mine. Now show me yours." My mouth dropped open.

"Emma Christine. Are you demanding that I drop this towel and walk back to my room naked to get my pajamas and let you watch the whole time?" I pretended to be horrified.

"Uh, yes? Have you seen yourself from the back?" I turned my head and attempted to do that, but ended up just going in a circle.

"I mean, not really because I'm not an owl and can't turn my head all the way around. I've caught glimpses in mirrors. I don't see anything to write home about." I mean, I didn't think my body was disgusting, but I didn't think it was the bomb either. Just . . . in between. I had parts I liked and parts I hated and I tried most of the time not to focus too much on the latter. I was old enough now that I knew that thinking too much about those perceived flaws was a waste of fucking time and wasn't going to make your knees not do that weird thing when you ran.

"Your body is beautiful. Don't ever doubt that. Haven't I told you you're beautiful a dozen times before?" I clutched the towel tighter.

"Yes, but it wasn't in this context."

"What context is that?"

"Naked context." She laughed.

"Just drop the towel and let me watch." I rolled my eyes and sighed with as much drama as I could.

"Fine, fine." I pulled off the towel and dropped it on the floor.

"Did I mention that I sleep naked?" I asked, before I pivoted on my toes and walked back to my bedroom.

"Wait, what?" Emma said, stumbling after me. It was a testament to how shocked she was because she went right by the towel I'd so carelessly flung on the floor without picking it up.

"Yeah, I've been not sleeping naked because I didn't want to go through a whole production when I went to the bathroom, but yeah. I prefer it. See, there are still some things you don't know about me." Very few, but I'd told her about two more of them tonight, so I was running low on secrets at the moment. I needed to get some more so Emma wouldn't know every single fucking thing about me.

"Are you going to sleep naked tonight?" she asked, while we both stood in my bedroom. Me, naked, her, not naked.

"Thinking about it. Do you have any opinions on whether I should or not?" I tapped my chin and pretended to think. "Should I sleep naked tonight? Hmmm . . ."

"This is the easiest question I've ever answered in my life. Yes, you should sleep naked. If you want to. If that's what you usually do. Have you seriously been sleeping naked all these years and I had no idea?" She almost looked like that emoji whose head was exploding.

"I mean, I didn't do it around you. That would have been weird. But I'm guessing it might not have been weird?" This whole night was weird, and I still didn't know where we were going with all of this. I could still feel the thrust of her fingers inside me and her teeth biting my lips.

"No, it would have been weird back then. I mean, for you."

I shivered a little bit. Maybe sleeping naked wasn't the best idea. I wanted to ask Emma what she meant by that, but then Vegas bounded into the room and started licking my legs and I decided that sleeping naked wasn't the best solution when you had a new puppy that was hyperactive and liked to lick things.

"Okay, not sleeping naked," I said, as Emma grabbed the puppy and kept him from jumping up on me and digging his little murder feet into my skin.

I pulled some undies, shorts, and a tank out of my drawers and put them on.

"Bummer," Emma said with a sigh, as she held Vegas.

"I'm sure you'll see me naked again."

"Will I?" she asked, and she looked so worried about what my answer would be.

"I mean, I guess? I don't know, Em. This all is happening really fast and I'm tired and I think I just need to shut down for a little while. Is that okay? I'll take the puppy though." I held out my arms for him and she passed him over.

"Yeah, yeah. That's fine." It definitely didn't sound fine, but I needed a break from all this. My entire world had been flipped on its axis and I was floating around in zero gravity and trying to figure out how to stand up again. That was going to take time and sleep and a lot of thinking and processing. I couldn't do that all in one night, and I didn't know how to tell Emma that now I needed space from her.

"It's a lot," I said, rubbing Vegas' ears. He loved having them rubbed for some reason.

"Yeah, fine," she said, but her face fell anyway. It hurt me that she was hurting, but I needed this and I hoped she would understand that.

"I need a snack," I said, putting my hand on my grumbling stomach. "Like right now. You hungry?"

"Maybe a little." I heard another stomach noise, and it wasn't mine. Hers was complaining too.

"Come on," I said, putting the puppy down. He bolted out the door and into the living room and I heard the frantic squeaking of a toy. We needed to remember to put away the noisy toys before we went to bed every night so he wouldn't sneak them out and then we'd hear them in the middle of the night.

"What are you going to make?" she asked as I stared into the pantry and then opened the fridge.

"It's time for . . ." I made my voice deep and intense. "Lazy Charcuterie." That was what I called it when I wanted to eat crackers and cheese for dinner. I didn't want to cook or do anything too complicated because I was tired and needed something fast.

"I have some brie, if you want." Of course she did. Emma always had the good stuff. I raided the fridge and she helped me set up a tray with a few different kinds of crackers, several cheeses, some pepperoni, some grapes, a few handfuls of nuts, and some small candy bars I'd found that I had probably stashed here in case of PMS.

"Classy AF," I said, looking at the creation. Emma arranged it much more artfully than I would have.

"Shall we?" I asked, picking up the tray. Emma got some seltzer waters and followed me to the couch. I put my feet up on the coffee table and tried to keep the food out of puppy reach.

"Maybe we should do this in bed. I'm having visions of him just flipping this entire thing and then us being really sad. Your room?" My bed was covered in sex sheets that I was going to need to change before I went to bed. I was definitely going to make Emma help me change them since she was partially responsible for them being sex sheets in the first place.

"Sure," she said, but I could sense hesitation, but she followed me with the drinks as Vegas frolicked happily along beside us, totally convinced that we had made an entire tray of delicious snacks for him. I was going to sneak him some pepperoni when Emma wasn't looking. I couldn't be a total monster and deny his sweet face.

We both climbed on Emma's bed and then Vegas whined to be let up.

"I don't think we're going to be able to do this with him up here." Emma pulled something out of her nightstand.

"That's why I have these stashed all over the house." It was a chew toy that might keep him busy long enough for us to inhale our snacks.

"Brilliant. Have I ever told you how much I envy your mind?" It must be so organized in there. Lots of shelves with labels. It probably looked like The Container Store with all her thoughts cataloged and in the right place.

"Maybe, but it's always nice to hear," she said, giving me

a soft smile. I dug into the cheese and crackers, just shoving them in my mouth indiscriminately. Emma, on the other hand, made little sandwiches and nibbled like a duchess, getting zero crumbs on the bed. We were such a contrast sometimes.

"Are we going to talk about what happened or no?" Emma asked, after she had a few of the cracker sandwiches and moved on to the grapes. I was alternating cheese, crackers, and pepperoni so I got a little bit of each, and tried not to get too many crumbs on the bed.

"I'm not ready, Em. I'm just not ready to talk about how I feel. This was all a massive shock to me. What you did and what I did and what we did together? It's too much to process all at once. I mean, have you been thinking about all that before?" I hadn't. Not in a concrete, tangible way.

"Yes," she said, popping a grape in her mouth.

"Okay, are you going to elaborate?" I asked, when she didn't add anything else.

"No," she said. "I don't think you're ready for that." I set down the two "fun size" (bullshit) candy bars that I'd been about to nom on and gave her my full attention.

"Ready for what?" My stomach knotted up a little, realizing that our friendship had completely changed and there was nothing we could do to put Pandora back in her box.

"That's because we were never talking about *this*."

"And what is this?" I gestured between us.

"I don't know," she said, after the longest pause in history.

"I don't either, but you've definitely thought about this longer than I have. That's pretty clear." Just how long? And why hadn't she said anything until tonight?

"It's complicated, Callyn. So complicated." She sealed her lips shut, as if she was blocking the tide of words that were going to spill out of she let them.

"Just talk to me. Tell me."

I reached out and took her hand, squeezing it. For some reason that action felt different now. Everything was different.

She made a sniffing noise and ducked her head.

"Hey, don't cry," I said, shoving the snacks aside so I could pull her into my arms. "There's no reason to cry, Em. You can tell me anything."

"I don't know if I can tell you this. I don't want to wreck everything." I patted her back and held her as tight as I could.

"You're not going to wreck everything." I mean, if having sex had wrecked anything, the damage was already done. But our relationship had been through so much already. We'd crossed time and distance away and we were still together. I couldn't foresee a future that Emma wasn't in. She was home for me, and I think it was the same for her. That didn't go away overnight.

"I'm scared," she said, and that was the root of things. She was scared that she was going to lose me, but that wasn't possible.

"You can never lose me, Emma. You are literally stuck with me forever. I'm not going anywhere. You're my go home."

"I'm scared it's going to change everything." I pulled back so she could look at me.

"Emma. You literally had your mouth on my junk. Everything has already changed. Now we have to make sense of it and the first thing to do is for you to talk to me." She sighed and reached for a tissue from her nightstand.

"I know. I know. And I'm sorry for being so weird now. Things were different when we were naked and I was making you scream." Chills broke out on my skin when I thought about all the ways she'd made me scream.

"Mmm, that was pretty good. But we need to talk about the stuff that happened before and after the screaming." Emma shredded a few tissues in her hand.

"I've been in love with you for our whole lives, Callyn. Both as a friend and as something else. I was in love with you before I even knew what that meant. I've . . . I've been holding onto this because I thought I would grow out of it, or I thought it would change, or I thought it would ruin what we had. I knew you didn't feel that way about me. Trust me, I looked for signs. I would have given anything for a sign from you that you felt the same way."

I was about ready to slide off the bed.

"You *love* me? As something other than a friend? Like, the sex was about you being sexually attracted to me? And you're romantically attracted to me too?" My voice squeaked because I was pretty much flipping out. You might as well have told me that the planet was actually called Xeron and the ocean was full of orange juice.

Emma shook her head at me.

"Callyn, you useless lesbian. I'm attracted to you in every way you can be attracted to another person." She laughed a little as I gaped at her.

"What is even happening right now? You *love* me?" I was losing my mind. This couldn't be real life.

"Yes, I love you. I've been in love with you forever. You just never noticed." There was no way I could be that dense. No way.

"You never said anything!" I screeched, throwing my hands in the air.

"I didn't want you to know!" she yelled back.

"What the fuck!" I screamed, and then I started laughing because this whole thing was beyond ridiculous.

"I don't know!" Now we were both yelling, and Vegas had started barking to join the mayhem.

"You love me?" I asked again, in a softer voice.

"Yeah, I do. I don't remember a time when I didn't. I don't know how to not love you, Cal." She leaned close and I dove deep into her eyes to see the absolute truth in them.

"That's a double negative," I said. "But I get what you mean. I think . . . I don't even know. I really don't." Was I in love with her? Surely not. I couldn't wrap my head around that concept. Of course I loved her as a friend, but that was it, right? I didn't love her all the other ways.

"It's okay. This is why I didn't want to tell you, because I knew it would freak you out and then I thought you might go running for the hills. We can't stay friends if one of us is in love with the other one. I could never lose you, Callyn. Never. That would destroy me and I'd never recover." Uh, same. Needing to do something with my hands, I started pulling grapes off the stems and then popping them in my mouth. I didn't even really like grapes, but it didn't matter.

"I'm not freaking out," I said, but then I realized I was squishing grapes with my hands.

"I think you're freaking out a little bit," Emma said, as she took the squished grapes out of my hands and then wiped them off with more tissues.

"Okay, fine. I'm freaking out. But only because I feel like everything I knew is wrong and now I have to readjust my entire fucking perception. And that's a lot." I was doing the exact thing she'd worried about me doing, thus proving her right.

"I've tried to tell you, so many times. So many damn times." She took the rest of the grapes away from me so I wouldn't massacre them too.

"And what stopped you?" I asked.

"This." She gestured between us. Right. She did have a point.

"But it must have been killing you all these years to hold

that secret, my god, Emma." That made me want to cry. She was keeping this enormous secret from me for our whole lives and had to deal with that every day.

"It wasn't easy. It hasn't been easy."

"You hid it so well." She rolled her eyes.

"Not well enough, I'm pretty sure all of our friends know. Actually, they definitely know." And *they* never said anything either? I really was a useless lesbian.

"Everything I knew is wrong," I said, and I started laughing again until I couldn't stop. I started choking on my own saliva and then it was all over after that.

Emma handed me one of the seltzer waters and I gulped it down before burping a few times.

"Sorry. I have no idea why you love me, I'm such a mess." Right after I said that, I slopped some seltzer water on myself. Emma patted me dry.

"You're a little bit of a mess. But you're my mess. Always have been. I don't mind a little mess. I think I need it to shake me up. Do you have any idea what my life would be like without you?"

"Cleaner?" I asked, brushing some crumbs off the bed and onto the floor.

"No. Boring. Colorless. Way too controlled. You're my surprise. You're my pizzazz. You're the sun hanging in the sky." Her words created a lump in my throat and I had to hold back tears.

"That's an awfully nice thing to say," I said, sniffing. Now it was my turn for tissues. Emma handed me the box and I blotted at the corners of my eyes.

"It's true. I don't know what shape my life would have been without you and I don't like thinking about it." Agreed. Emma had always been present, even when she was miles away, or we hadn't talked in weeks. I'd hear her voice in the back of my mind, I'd write down lists of jokes and other things I wanted to tell her and then I'd send these long emails and messages that I know she read every word of because she would send similar long emails back. Emma was knit completely and totally into my life and she always would be.

"I just love you, Callyn. Always have, always will." Now I was crying again. What a night this had been. It was beyond late and Vegas had passed out again and I needed to go to work tomorrow, but none of those other things mattered.

"I love you. I'm not sure what that means right now. Can I take some time and figure it out?" I asked. She nodded and rubbed my arm.

"Yeah, you can. Just keep talking to me and asking any questions. I'm sorry that I didn't tell you until now. Until I had to."

I laughed. "Yeah, the sex kind of made this conversation inevitable. Speaking of that, it was really good right? I mean, holy shit. You are good at sex and we are good at sex together." That made her blush and giggle. She was so damn cute.

"Yeah, it was pretty awesome. But we probably shouldn't do it again until you figure out your feelings, right? And then there's the whole fact that we're married." Oh, shit, I had completely forgotten about that part. It was kind of hilarious when you thought about it.

"Now I'm beginning to see how we ended up married in Vegas if you've been secretly in love with me all this time. You sure you didn't instigate it?"

"I don't remember anything," she said, a little too quickly, but instead of calling her out, I decided to let that one go for tonight. It was so fucking late and I was so tired.

"I think I should sleep in my room and you should sleep in yours and we should both be clothed, yes?" I picked up the tray, fully intending to bring it back to my room with me. I was still hungry.

"Excuse me, where are you going with that?" she asked.

"I'm taking this back to my room where I'm going to finish it. I can't let this go to waste. That would be shameful." Emma hopped off the bed and tried to take the tray from me. I had to dance around her to get out of her reach.

"No, my snacks!" I growled at her and she just stopped and narrowed her eyes.

"You are ridiculous when it comes to food. I guess I'll let you get away with this. Once. But never again." She pointed at me and left the room, presumably to go to the kitchen and get her own snacks.

"That wasn't mean, was it?" I asked, looking down at the passed-out Vegas. He was such a weird sleeper sometimes. He'd either sleep with his back bent so far, I was worried for his spine, or he'd sleep flat on his stomach with his legs out at all angles. Neither position looked that comfortable.

I went to my room with the tray and was hit in the chest by the rumpled bed. It didn't smell like sex in here anymore, or at least I didn't think it did. I put the tray down on my dresser and stripped the bed, chucking the sheets in the corner. I'd wash them at some point. I pulled the extra sheets out from the closet and spent a few sweaty minutes wrestling them back onto the bed. The pillows were still dented from our heads. I stripped the cases and fluffed them a few times to make them puffy again.

Vegas ran in and cried to get on the bed and I gave in and then gave him two pepperonis to munch on as I finished the rest of the snack tray standing up.

There was a knock at the door and I had my mouth full, so it took a few tries before I could say "come in."

"You'd better not be feeding him people food." Vegas and I looked at each other and then at Emma.

"I would never do that," I said, and Vegas barked, as if he was agreeing with me. "See?"

Emma shook her head.

"So, I'm going to bed and it would feel weird if I didn't say goodnight, so . . . goodnight? Uh, I'll see you tomorrow?" She saluted me and I started to laugh. "I'm sorry, I don't know why I did that. It was weird." She spun around and left before I could say anything. I wanted to say goodnight too. I heard the water going in the bathroom and I saw the door was open.

"You didn't let me say goodnight," I said, and she jumped, her toothbrush in her mouth.

"You scared me," she said, through a mouthful of toothpaste.

"Sorry. But goodnight. You didn't let me say it." I saluted her as well and she rolled her eyes and spit into the sink.

"You're ridiculous."

"And you love it," I said, twirling around.

"Yes, I do." She said it quiet enough that I didn't think she wanted me to hear.

Chapter Eleven

I MADE Vegas stay with me the whole night and I think he got tired of me nervously petting him, so he went to the end of the bed and laid on my feet, but he did stay with me.

I couldn't sleep. It was impossible to be in a bed that only hours ago I'd been fucking my best friend in. How did I see this bed for sleeping when it had been used for that? I couldn't get comfortable and I couldn't stop thinking about the sounds she'd made and how she tasted and how she said she'd always been in love with me.

Honestly? I was kinda pissed. How dare she keep that secret from me for this many years? I mean what the *fuck*. I kept searching my memories, looking for clues. So far I didn't have any. Was it possible that I had missed all the signs? My friends hadn't, so Emma had said. I needed to have a serious chat with all of them and ask what they were thinking when they didn't tell me how obvious it was that Emma was in love with me.

What had I missed? And what did it mean for me? What happened now? How could I be only friends with her if she was wanting something more? That wasn't fair to either of us. And if I decided that I was in love with her, was it real, or did I just think that because I wanted to make her happy because she was my best friend?

Too many questions and I had zero answers. So I spent most of the night turning everything over and over in my head, like socks in a dryer. I had no answers by the time I passed out, right before my alarm went off.

Today was going to fucking suck.

∽

I NEEDED a coffee IV to get through the day, but that wasn't going to happen, so I just stopped and got a Venti pumpkin crème cold brew after dropping Vegas off at doggie daycare. Emma was sleeping in and mumbled goodbye to me when I left. It wasn't like her to sleep in, so I was a little worried, but she answered when I texted her later and didn't seem any different, so who knew.

I sucked my coffee down so fast that I swear I started vibrating on the street.

"How much coffee have you had today, my goodness," Jessika said, when I was pouring myself another cup during my morning break. My hands were shaking, but I had to stay awake today or else I wasn't going to make it through. Yes, I was leaving in less than three days, but I was training my replacement and she wouldn't stop asking questions and I needed to be alert to tell her the answers. I didn't want my employer to pull something and not pay me because I'd mentally checked out. That sounded like something they would do. My replacement, Maggie, was . . . eager. She was also young and wanted to do a really, really good job and I wanted to tell her that she needed to tone it down and also not to give this place her everything because they would chew her up and spit her out, just like it did to me. But I didn't think she'd listen to me, so I went ahead and just took all of her questions and tried to keep the editorializing to myself.

I realized Jessika was waiting for an answer. I sucked in a mouthful of coffee before I answered. I hadn't even added any cream or sugar or anything and it was awful but I didn't need anything impeding the caffeine getting into my body.

"Uh, enough," I said, in answer to her question. My lips were trembling.

"Yeah, you're going to need to put that cup down, babe," she said, taking it from me. I resisted for a second, but let her take the cup from me. She stepped closer and examined me.

"Your entire face is twitching. Why have you been downing the coffee today? Rough night? I hope it was fun." Uh, that would be one word for it, I guess? The sex was fun, more than fun, but the other stuff wasn't so great.

"Uh, just had a lot . . . on my mind and didn't sleep and I need to keep myself peppy for the new girl and I think I ordered a coffee that was too large and drank it really fast and here we are." Even I could tell I was speaking at a speed too fast for another human to follow.

"Water. Right now. You aren't going to be any good at anything when you're in hyper speed like this." She was probably right. I poured the coffee down the sink and then took a few breaths before I went back to my desk. I told Maggie to take a break herself, but she said she didn't want to (what?), and was at the desk reading through the employee manual again.

"Hey! You got a few calls," she said, and I didn't know if I could deal with much more of her enthusiasm. I was just so tired. Wired and tired at the same time. It wasn't a fun state to be in.

I grabbed my water bottle and gulped some down while

Maggie prattled away. There was a tap on my shoulder. I turned around to find Jessika looking down at me.

"Hey, can I grab you for a second? I need to ask you something." I excused myself from Maggie, who looked like she wanted to follow me but didn't, and walked after Jessika back to the break room.

"We didn't finish our conversation. And you have ten more minutes for your break, so spill." She leaned on the counter and I copied her pose.

"Uh, well . . . some things happened?" I wasn't sure if I wanted to talk to her about this because I was still trying to work through it all myself. I didn't need other input confusing me further.

"What kind of things?"

"Let's just say a lot of things changed and now my world has been rocked and I'm struggling to deal with the fallout. And I'm confused and things are awkward and I don't know what to do." Jessika's eyebrows rose.

"You going to elaborate on that?"

I shook my head.

"I can't. Not yet. It's still too much and I don't even know what to say."

"Okay, fine. I'd say just take some time away from . . . whatever is confusing you. Try to pull your emotions out of it and think if this situation were happening to your best friend, what advice would you give her? Be as kind and loving to yourself as you'd be with someone you love." I started laughing when she mentioned the part about the best friend, and she was looking at me as if I had lost my mind. I probably had. Must be all the caffeine.

"I'm sorry. I'm fine." It was a lot of effort to stifle the giggles and stop laughing. I took a deep breath and tried to find my center. My center was hopped up on too much caffeine. It was like I had pissed-off bees buzzing in my veins.

"Okay, I think you should go home. Seriously. You only have a few days left, what are they going to do to you? Do you have any sick days left?" I hadn't really kept track.

"I'm not sure." Jessika marched me back to my computer and made me check. I had one day left of sick time, somehow.

"Okay, you're going home," she said, and made me punch out, said she would put Maggie with Linda to work on another project, and pushed me toward the staff room where we stored our coats and bags.

I didn't realize I had really left until I was standing on the street and people were pushing past me.

I couldn't remember the last time I had free hours in the middle of a weekday. What kind of luxury was this? There were so many possibilities and I still had so much caffeine in my body. First up, I think I needed to walk some of the caffeine off, so I took myself up the street to a juice bar and got one that was supposed to detox you, which was probably bullshit, but vegetables were always good, so I sucked it down and grabbed some weird cookies they had at the counter that were vegan and surprisingly delicious.

After sucking down some more water, I could feel myself finally starting to crash from the caffeine wearing off, so I headed to Boston Common for a brisk walk through the gardens and around the pond. I stopped to talk to a few ducks and then tried to decide where to go. I was broke as fuck, so shopping was out. I realized where I was and then I knew my destination: the library. It didn't matter if you were broke at the library. They'd still let you take out books.

It had been a long time since I'd been there, so I let myself wander, stopping briefly to sit in the garden in the middle of the building, and then trying to decide what I wanted. There were a few new releases that I'd been wanting to get, so I headed that way first, and had to stop myself from getting too many because my backpack was only so big, and my back was only so strong.

I wandered some more and found myself (somehow) in the self-help section. I didn't believe in book shame, but this was not really the place I wanted to end up. I started to turn around and leave, but something told me to keep looking, so I did. I scanned the shelves and pulled out anything that struck my fancy. I picked up a book about money (I definitely needed some major help there, but that was mostly due to capitalism and having too much student loan debt), and then I ended up in the relationship area. Yikes.

I skimmed through a bunch, but most of the ones I found were . . . very heterosexual. I didn't need to know how to communicate with a man. Frustrated, I tried a few more and realized that I was looking for answers when there weren't any right now. None of these books had this exact situation in them. The advice in these pages was probably something along the lines of "suck it up and talk to Emma, you idiot."

I knew if I told someone else what had happened, that's what they would say. I loved Jessika's advice to give myself the advice I would give someone I love. We were always hardest on ourselves. That led me to stroll down a different aisle and then to another area of the library where I asked myself what would happen if the roles were reversed. What would I tell Emma to do if she were me?

What if I had been the one in love with her and then everything had happened? That was something to think about. I had to sit down in a corner in a plush leather chair that was so big that I felt like it encased me. There weren't a whole lot of people in this part of the library so it was relatively quiet, but I was getting itchy, so I got out my earbuds and put on some music that I could tune out if I needed to, but would help with the annoyance I had with silence. I also had a fidget cube in my bag and got that out to give my hands something to do.

Now I was imagining myself if I'd been in love with Emma my whole life. Had pined and wished and wanted her from afar and never gotten the courage to tell her because I was afraid of ruining what we had as friends. My head was definitely exploding again. Even though I was sitting down, I still felt like I was going to fall over somehow. I dropped the cube and my hands gripped the arms of the chair so hard I thought my nails were going to tear the leather. That would be a shame, so I let up, but I couldn't calm my racing heart. It was definitely out of my control right now. I also had a floating sensation, as if I wasn't completely tethered to my body. I looked at my hands, but were they my hands?

The song I was listening to ended and another began, and it made me jump because it was a switch from a calm folk song to a louder and more aggressive pop song. I yanked out my earbuds and I was glad that no one was around to see me having a complete and total breakdown. If I was a car, I could call someone to come and fix this, but I wasn't, so I was going to have to handle this myself.

I called on all of my meditation skills, but it took quite a while for me to be able to breathe in a normal way and get my heart to slow the fuck down.

Once I was out of the woods, I tried to figure out what the hell had happened. I had just flipped out and I wasn't sure why.

Emma. Thinking about Emma. Thinking about being in love with Emma. I wasn't, but even thinking about it was . . . something.

I wasn't in love with Emma. No, I wasn't. Now I was arguing with myself. At least I wasn't saying anything out loud. Muttering to myself might get me thrown out of the library, but maybe not. That probably wasn't the worst thing that had happened in the Boston Public Library. Ew. I didn't want to think about other things that had happened here.

I needed to move. I needed to pace and think again, so I got up and put on my backpack, full-o-books, and left, not even caring where I was going, but then I realized I was headed toward the ocean. I could smell the salt hanging in the air and it always made me feel like I was safe. I couldn't explain it, but whenever my life was shitty, I wanted to smell and be near the sea. Too bad I was too broke to head to the Cape like other people. Maybe after Lara's wedding we could all plan a group trip. Then it wouldn't be so expensive if we split renting a place together.

I walked as close to the water as I could get and let the salty breeze tease my hair, blowing it all over my face. I closed my eyes and breathed deep. Now it was time to organize my thoughts about Emma.

I wish I could do this with Emma. She was the one who helped take what was in my brain and turn into something coherent. Sometimes I just needed to talk some tangled thing out to her and she would sit and listen to me, even if I wasn't asking her to say anything. She was always like that, and I gave her great advice that I would never follow myself. I gave her better advice than I'd give myself because I cared about her more.

We were best friends. I loved her the way a best friend did. Right?

Sure, I got little flutters in my chest when she came in the room, but that was because she made me happy. That didn't have anything to do with romance. I got flutters when I saw pizza too. I didn't want to fuck or marry pizza. Well. Maybe I could marry pizza if I wasn't already married to Emma. Right. I kept forgetting about that somehow.

It didn't have to mean anything, being married to Emma. I was sure that people who were best friends had gotten married before and it wasn't for romantic or sexual or any other reasons. We'd just gotten drunk, and I bet there had been plenty of those.

It all came down to this: did I love Emma as something other than a friend? I still didn't know. How did you know if you were in love with someone other than as a friend? Where was the book on *that*? I pulled out my phone and did a quick search. I read through a few lists, but most of the things were also best friendship things. Weren't they?

You were supposed to put your best friend above your others. That was what made her a best friend. So what if I loved touching her hair. So what if we'd already fucked and it was amazing and I couldn't stop thinking about it? SO WHAT?!

I was getting nowhere, so I put on a podcast and started walking again. I might as well pick up Vegas and go home. It would be nice to see him and relax in the apartment for a little bit. I could even make dinner for Emma, or at least try. If it didn't work out, I could always order food and then pretend I made it. She would let me get away with that because apparently she was in love with me.

I couldn't figure out why, but I guess that wasn't my job. My only task was figuring out how I felt about her. I didn't really want to, honestly, because I knew when I did, everything would really, definitively change. We were in a strange sort of limbo right now, not knowing how to be around each other, but at some point, that limbo would lead somewhere.

I couldn't lose her. No matter what. I couldn't live a life without Emma in it. What would be the point?

~

THEY WERE surprised when I came and got Vegas, but he greeted me as if we hadn't seen each other in three thousand years instead of just a few hours. It was a struggle to get the wiggly puppy and my backpack full of books home in one piece, but I made it. The first thing I did when I let Vegas off his leash was grab some treats. We were working on training and I wanted to be really good at it. I wanted him to be the valedictorian of the puppy training class. Emma would probably say that we'd be happy as long as he just did his best, but I wanted him to be the best instead. Wipe the floor with those other loser puppies.

"Sit," I said to Vegas. He was working on this one. I tried a few times and finally rewarded him when he sat with one of his new favorite treats. He chomped it down so fast that I thought he was going to choke.

"Calm down there, puppy," I said, as he whined for more treats. I made him sit again and gave him another, but that was it. I distracted him from begging me for more by getting his loudest toy and throwing it across the room for him to chase. I burst out laughing when he skidded on the slick floor in his attempt to barrel after the toy. So cute and so enthusiastic.

I made myself a cup of herbal tea and fixed a quick snack as I unpacked my library books. I wanted to read them all at once, but that was physically impossible, so I sat down with the one that I wanted to read the most and cracked it open, completely ignoring the stack of books I'd bought with Emma on the day we'd gotten Vegas. I set a timer for myself because if I didn't, I'd get completely lost in the world and be here reading for the next ten hours straight.

Vegas danced around with his toy and every now and then I'd look up and throw it for him. I couldn't remember an afternoon like this during a weekday in forever. My new job had better vacation time, so I was definitely going to make days like this a priority in the future. Getting things done was important, but so was taking time to do a whole lot of nothing.

An hour later, I reluctantly put a bookmark between the pages and set the book down. It was one of the hardest things I'd ever had to do. The book was everything I wanted it to be and there wasn't a dull moment to take a break, but I had stopped myself anyway. I had a quick stretch break and then went to the kitchen to figure out how to make an impressive dinner for when Emma came home. I always wanted to impress her because I felt like I failed so often at everything.

We had shrimp and chicken and peppers and kale and rice and quinoa and limes and barbecue sauce and a spice cabinet full of everything you could possibly want. I put a bunch of the ingredients into a search engine and decided to make barbecue shrimp over rice on a bed of kale. Healthy and delicious. I could pull this off, I was sure.

～

EMMA WALKED in the door just as I had started to cry.

"What are you doing home?" she asked, and then she saw my tears and immediately dropped her backpack and came over to hug me.

"I'm sorry. I left work early because I had too much caffeine and then I was trying to make dinner and I ruined everything somehow." I gestured to the burned shrimp and gluey rice. At least the kale was okay, but all I'd had to do was wash and put that on a plate.

"Aw, it's okay. We can have chicken on a salad. It's all defrosted and everything. Don't worry. Thank you for making dinner for me." She rubbed my back and soothed my tears and I sniffed and tried to get my shit together. I didn't know why little things going wrong always upset me more than bigger things.

"It's fine," I said, wiping my eyes. "I don't know why I'm making such a big deal of things. I'm just being dramatic." Emma squeezed my shoulders and looked down at the burned shrimp.

"You're not. I remember when I was learning how to cook and I ruined an entire lasagna and I felt so horrible because the ingredients weren't cheap and it was completely inedible. It's okay, we can buy more shrimp. And maybe I have been remiss in not teaching you how to cook." I shook my head.

"No, that's on me. I'm a grown fucking adult and I should have learned on my own. Just because my parents didn't want to teach me doesn't mean I couldn't get on the internet and figure it out." In fact, I was going to do that. There were plenty of videos online that would break it down so simply so that a child could follow them. I could at least handle that.

Emma tossed the ruined food and I scrubbed out the pans in the sink as she got the chicken started in a pan with some lime juice and spices. She asked me to cut up some peppers, so I did that.

"How was your day?" I asked, because she'd been conspicuously silent.

"Good. I have a huge test next week, so I'm probably going to have my nose in the textbooks this weekend. Sorry."

"That's fine," I said, trying not to chop my finger off. "Just let me know when you need breaks and I'll bring you tea and take your mind off it. I can quiz you too." Emma was a huge fan of flash cards and I had quizzed her dozens of times before.

"Sounds good. I'll probably hit you up for that on Sunday."

We lapsed into silence again and I could feel the tension in the room.

"Everything okay?" I asked. She turned around and gave me a startled look.

"Yeah, why?"

"Um, because of last night? And we're not being like we usually are." She stared at the chicken, pretending that she had to watch it as if that was the most important task in the world.

"What do you mean?" Okay, now she was just being obtuse. I sighed and she glanced up at me.

"You know what I mean, Emma. We had sex and you told me you loved me and now things are weird, which is probably why you waited for so long to tell me that you loved me in the first place. You probably could have done that without the sex, even though the sex was . . ." I trailed off because my brain tended to shut down when I thought about the sex. I'd done my best *not* to think about it because when I did, I forgot everything I was doing, including how to breathe. I dove headfirst into my memories and my face flushed and it became uncomfortable to be around people. Like they could see me thinking lusty thoughts about my best friend.

It was happening right now and I had to snap myself out of it.

"Are you okay? You look like you're stoned. I've never seen you stoned, but this is probably what you would look like." As she said it, I could feel my cheeks heat and I had to stare down at the peppers.

"I'm fine," I said, chopping the peppers into smaller pieces.

"No you're not, tell me." This was probably a derailing tactic, but whatever. If she really wanted to know, I'd tell her.

"I was thinking about what it was like fucking you. I can't

stop thinking about it. I messed up so much stuff at work and the new girl had to keep asking me if I was okay because I'd trail off in the middle of a sentence because I was thinking about you."

I wanted to see her face when I said it, so I made sure I was staring right into her eyes. They were a mix of blue-green right now.

Emma and I stared at each other for seconds that felt like years. Like eternity. Something shifted between us and I couldn't even breathe. I had forgotten how, and it didn't seem important in this moment. I nearly swallowed my tongue when the sound of the smoke alarm startled both of us.

"Shit," Emma said, ripping the smoking pan of chicken off the stove and throwing it into the sink before running to the smoke detector with a dish towel and waving it until the beeping stopped. Vegas decided to join the mayhem and howl, so I picked him up to comfort him and then open a window to get the scent of burned chicken and burned shrimp out of the apartment.

"We're going to get evicted," I said, as I came back into the kitchen to find Emma scraping the chicken into the trash. "Order pizza?" I suggested, setting Vegas down. He was still barking, but it wasn't as loud.

"Vegas, chill out," I said, and he looked at me with confusion. "The barking is not helping. See, it's okay now." The smell of burned things was starting to dissipate as Emma leaned on the counter.

"This is exactly what I was hoping to avoid. I never should have kissed you and started this. I should have left things alone." I went to her and pulled her into my arms. Her hair smelled like burned chicken. Mine probably smelled like burned shrimp. At least I wasn't the only one who had screwed up dinner. I was still starving, but comforting Emma was more important right now.

"To be fair, I kissed you back. I'm not really sure how the sex started, but it did start and I wanted it. I just don't know what that means. Does it mean that my feelings for you are more than platonic? Does it mean I just really needed to get laid? I don't know, Emma. I need to figure it out and I don't know how to do that. I even looked at some self-help books at the library today, but they were way too heterosexual." I pulled back and made a face and she laughed. She was crying again too.

"Everything is way too heterosexual."

"True."

We stared at each other again and it was as if the earth had taken a breath and decided to pause on its axis to give us this chance to look at each other.

"Let's order pizza and just be us. Let's be Callyn and Emma again," I said, running my fingers through her hair and wiping her tears with my fingers. She sniffed.

"What does that mean?"

"Let's find out." The only way out was through, and we were going to get through this. We'd already walked through fire together, our hands clasped tight to one another. This was an obstacle we could overcome.

At least that was what I was going to keep telling myself.

Chapter Twelve

WE DID END up ordering pizza, but we also finished making the kale salads so at least we didn't have to order those.

"Who knew that potatoes would be good on pizza?" I asked, as I went for my third piece. The toppings also included scallions, bacon, and ranch dressing. Don't knock it until you try it.

"These people did, that's for sure," Emma said. We had a trashy reality show on that we'd seen already, but still loved to watch and mock and enjoy.

Vegas was asleep again. He seemed to only have two settings and I wondered if that would change as he got older. I kind of hoped that it didn't, but we weren't sure how big he was going to get, and I couldn't imagine his energy inside a bigger dog. Right now he was just a *tiny* menace.

Emma picked at her salad and I could tell she was having difficulty with trying to be how we used to be. It would take practice and I didn't want to leave her hanging either. I was going to figure this shit out. I watched her eat her pizza and asked myself if I was in love with her and it was like my brain made a popping noise and broke. Like thinking about her was too much for me to handle and I overloaded every time I tried. Maybe writing it down would work? I was going to try that when I was alone in bed tonight.

"Can you stop staring at me?" she asked, and I blinked and realized that I had been staring at her.

"Sorry. I was lost in thought."

"What kind of thoughts?" She pulled a thin slice of potato off the pizza and ate it. I'd never seen Emma disassemble her food before. That was something I usually did.

"Can we not do this right now? I just want to have dinner with you and watch crappy TV and talk like we always talk. I need time, Emma. I just need time." Pleading entered my voice and now my emotions were threatening to spill over.

I was completely overwhelmed.

"I'm sorry," she said, sniffling a little and then starting to dismantle another piece of pizza.

"I'm sorry too. This is just a weird situation and you've been thinking about it for years and years and I've been thinking of it for less than twenty-four hours. I need time to catch up. Time to breathe. Time to think." She nodded and stared at her pizza.

"Do you need that time away from me?" Her voice quivered and I realized that was one thing she was afraid of. That I was going to bail on her.

"No. Definitely not. I just need time away from all that to get my shit together. You know me, it takes longer than most." I didn't think I'd ever feel like I had my shit together. Maybe when I was eighty, and I would celebrate that day. "You're not getting rid of me that easily, Em." I reached out and squeezed her foot.

"Good," she said, and then folded the pizza in half and shoved most of it in her mouth. Guess we were good. Vegas woke up with a yip, as if he was upset to be awake. Same, puppy. Same.

WE FINISHED our pizza and were lounged on the couch when Emma started tilting her head from side to side and rubbing the back of her neck with her fingers.

"Do you need some help over there?" I asked.

"No, I'm good. I just have a little stress hanging out in my neck." Yeah, no wonder.

"Come on, turn around." I motioned for her to do so and she scooted so her back was facing me.

"Hold on just a second," I said, hopping up and running to my room. I came back with some CBD moisturizer and a little bottle of lavender essential oil. I mixed the two in my palms and started rubbing her neck and shoulders. I had to move her shirt aside and this would have been a lot easier if she was wearing a tank top. Or nothing at all.

This might have been a mistake. As soon as I started rubbing and digging into her muscles and feeling how warm and soft her skin was and hearing the little sounds of pleasure she made, I was instantly turned on and feeling pretty uncomfortable in my downstairs area. Even my nipples were tingling and I didn't think that was a thing. I thought it was made up.

"That feels really good," Emma said, and I tried to focus on rubbing the knots out of her neck without moving my hands lower or ripping off her shirt. I wanted to do both of those things more than I wanted to breathe right now.

Emma leaned back against me and leaned her head forward to give me more access to her neck.

"This would be easier if you took your shirt off," I blurted out. That was a thought that was supposed to stay in my head. Oops?

"Okay," she said, and a second later she wasn't wearing a shirt. She had a bra on, so that was a blessing, or a curse, depending. I gasped a little and choked on some of my own saliva that flooded my mouth as if Emma was something delicious I wanted to devour.

"Everything okay?" she asked, looking at me over her shoulder. She had an innocent look, but I wasn't fooled. She was trying to seduce me, and I was going to let her. After that talk of giving me space, Emma was using her wiles on me. I had to admire her shamelessness.

"Yup, fine," I said, managing to clear my throat and start my lungs working again. I'd seen Emma in a bra many, many times before, but never under quite these circumstances.

I put my fingers on her skin and she leaned into me more, begging for my fingers to touch her.

"I'm just going to move this," I said. Two could play this game. I could seduce her right back. I'd never thought of myself as a seductress, but whatever I'd done last time had worked, so I was going to go with this. I didn't want to be the only one who was uncomfortable.

I dug my fingers into her muscles, really working hard to get rid of the tension she stored there. She moaned and I just massaged harder. Good to know that she didn't mind if I treated her like a piece of clay I was mad at.

I put more lotion and oil on my hands and moved to her other shoulder, even though she hadn't asked me to work on that one. She wasn't complaining. My fingers moved further down her back, and she leaned forward to give me better access.

"This is getting in my way, so I'm going to take it off," I said, and gave her a minute to protest before I undid the hooks on her bra and pushed it out of my way. She let the straps fall fully down her arms and then pulled it all the way off. This moment had certainly escalated and I wondered which one of us was going to tap out first, or if that would even happen. Not going to lie, I was ready for sex again.

Sure, I'd said I needed time to think about what my feelings were, but I could also do that while fucking Emma. I was a multi-tasker.

I moved lower and lower on Emma's back until there wasn't anywhere else for me to go so I went back up and she looked at me again.

"Touch me," she said. I held up my hands.

"What have I been doing this whole time?" Thanks a lot, Emma. You're welcome for the massage.

"No, I want you to touch me in other places." She'd dropped the stealth and was playing her hand.

"What places? You're going to have to be very specific, because I might end up touching your nose if you don't give me the right direction." I stroked her nose with a finger and she inhaled shakily.

"Is it weird that's turning me on?" she asked. I laughed.

"Do you have something for noses? I bet we can pull up some nose porn if you're into that." She pretended to gag.

"No, thank you. I'm good. But I would rather have you touching some places other than my nose." She turned and we were face-to-face on the couch and I saw her in all her topless glory. Her tits really were ideal. Round and heavy and perfect.

"I'm going to need some direction, or I'm going for your nose again," I said, raising one finger and going at her with it.

"No, don't you dare!" I tackled her and started booping her nose repeatedly.

"Is this turning you on? Is this turning you on?" I asked as she laughed and squirmed under me. This position was really making her boobs move and I was mesmerized. I stopped poking her nose and stared down at her.

"See something you like?" she asked.

"Two somethings. Yes, I like them very much. Too much,

probably." Without her even asking, I stroked one of her breasts. I couldn't resist.

"Was this what you wanted me to touch?" Her eyes closed and she arched into me.

"Yes, please, yes." That was a good enough answer for me. I wanted to put lotion on her and give her another massage, but I also wanted to lick her all over, and that probably wouldn't taste good, so I refrained. They probably made edible lotion, but I didn't have any on hand. I made a mental note to look it up later. Much later.

"Is this interfering with your thinking?" she asked, as I lightly squeezed one of her breasts and then pinched one nipple. She made a little yelping noise of pleasure.

"Not at all," I said. "Not at all." I played and teased her nipples and soaked in her sounds of pleasure. I could pretty much do this all the time for the rest of my life and be happy. This was like grown-up sensory play. Plus, she enjoyed it, so there was that bonus. I loved making her feel good. I felt like I'd wasted too much time not touching her this way and I had to make up for it.

"I love it when you touch me like this. And I love the look on your face. Like I'm the most beautiful thing you've ever seen." I smiled down at her and swirled my finger around her belly button.

"You *are* the most beautiful thing I've ever seen." She smiled back at me and my heart felt too hot and too large to fit in my chest. I wasn't lying or exaggerating or flattering her. She was. I'd always thought so. I'd always been a little jealous of how gorgeous she was and wished I could look like her.

"Thank you," she said. Instead of arguing with me, or pointing out her own flaws, she just thanked me. That was something I needed to work on. I was awful at accepting compliments.

"I can't believe we're doing this again," I said. I mean, I could. I'd been thinking about it happening since it had happened last night. Had it only been one day? Time was a construct, so maybe it was more time than that. Or less. Who cared? It didn't matter, only now mattered.

"This wasn't my plan," she said, taking one of my hands and entwining our fingers. She brought my hand to her mouth and kissed it.

"It wasn't? With that whole performance about the stiff neck? I mean, come on. How much porn have you seen?" She raised one dark eyebrow.

"How much porn have *you* seen?" I really wanted to know what kind of porn she watched all of a sudden. She hadn't told me last night and now I wanted to know.

"My fair share. Sometimes I need a little stimulation, you know?" I did. In fact, I usually needed something like porn to really get myself in the sexy mindset. My ADHD brain needed something to focus on so I wasn't bouncing all around to other things and never having an orgasm. Porn was focus for me.

"What kind of porn do you watch?" I asked, and her cheeks got red. "Is it something . . . interesting?" I didn't want to kinkshame her at all. But I was definitely going to be a little hesitant if what got her off was like . . . blueberry girl porn, which was something I wish I had never looked up on the internet.

"Like, is it something I would be ashamed to tell you about?" she asked, and I nodded. "I don't think so? You wanna look at my search history?" Not really. All this talk of porn was riling me up and I wanted to be fucking rather than talking about watching other people fucking.

"We can chat about it post-coitus," I said.

"So there's going to be coitus?" she asked.

"Uh, yes? I mean, unless you don't want there to be. But

I figure that was where this was going. Did you want to stop?"

Emma shook her head.

"No, I don't want you to stop. But I really want you to take your clothes off. And I'm not sure if I want to do this on the couch. It's hard to clean cushions." Good point. So practical, that Emma.

"Okay, so bedroom? Wanna do yours this time?" Her bed was bigger and nicer than mine. I wanted to screw in luxury.

"Sure," she said, and got off the couch. Vegas woke up and started yipping. Emma looked at me in horror.

"We can't do anything in front of him. It would be too weird. We don't want to scar him." I started laughing as I gathered up every single one of his favorite toys and put them in the corner of the living room with his bed that he never used except for naps.

"He's a dog, Em. I'm sure he's seen humping before." He was still too young to get fixed, but it was happening as soon as he was old enough. I couldn't let my dog be a deadbeat dad, abandoning puppies right and left.

"Still. It just seems wrong." I made sure to distract Vegas while she picked up her shirt and bra and headed to her bedroom.

"You coming?" she asked, as I threw the ball for Vegas.

"Yes, and so will you," I said, and she rolled her eyes.

"You're shameless."

"Yes, thank you for noticing." I followed her into the bedroom and closed the door. Hopefully Vegas was amused or would fall asleep again. I didn't want any interruptions.

I leaned my back against the door.

"So," I said.

"So," she said, facing me. "You going to take your clothes off?"

"Eventually. I'd rather see you all the way naked first." She walked closer to me and my mouth got dry at the way she moved. Like she knew what she wanted and she was going to get it. I hoped I was what she wanted.

"No, I think *you* should get completely naked first." She started pulling at the hem of my shirt. I'd changed into more comfortable clothes this afternoon, so I didn't have much on anyway.

I closed my eyes and tried to breathe. She had me completely at her mercy as her fingers brushed my belly and she pulled my shirt over my head. I wasn't wearing a bra. Why bother when it was just the two of us?

"Mmm, yes, that's what I wanted to see," she said, running her hands across my collarbone. "You're still wearing too much, though." With one yank, she undid the tie of my shorts and then I was naked before I could say her name.

"God, your body is so perfect." She took my hand and led me to the bed and then pushed me down on it. She stood there, watching me, and I wondered if I should be doing anything. I wanted to be sexy, but I didn't know how.

"Do you know how hard it was to be in class today? To read about rat castration and try and take notes?" I shuddered.

"Can you not talk about rat castration when we're doing stuff like this? It doesn't really get me in the mood. Does it get you in the mood?" That was a horrifying thought. She laughed and went to turn on her salt lamp, light some candles, and then put on some music.

"Definitely not. I figured we could take our time and not rush tonight." We did kind of rush a little last time. But it was our first time together, so that was bound to happen.

"Slow," I said.

"Yes. Slow." She blew out a match and walked over to me.

"So slow you're going to beg. I'm very much looking forward to hearing you plead." Holy shit. She was going to kill me. I couldn't survive this night. Last time I was so caught up in the newness and the shock of it all that I wasn't really thinking about much except freaking out and hoping I didn't screw anything up or cause her to stop what she was doing. Tonight was different.

"Why are you doing this to me?" I asked in a hushed voice.

"Because I can. Because I've thought about doing this with you for years and years and I've got a lot of ideas and plans and things I've been waiting on." Oh. That made sense. I'd only had a few hours of fantasizing and she'd had years. I felt my entire body go red thinking about her thinking about me.

"And what did you think about?" I asked, not even sure if I wanted to know the answer.

"Just about everything," she said. "Some things more than others. But I want to do nearly everything with you." My mind caught on one word.

"Nearly?" I asked as she walked toward me again.

"I'm sure there are things you wouldn't want to do. There are things I don't want to do." Right now, I was most interested in the things she *did* want to do.

"What are you going to do first?" That was the most pressing question. I was still lying on the bed naked, propped up on my elbows so I could watch her.

"First? First I'm going to kiss you." That seemed like a very good place to start.

"Kiss me, then," I said.

"Just one more thing." Before I knew she was doing it, she was stripping out of her pants and we were both naked. That was better and it gave me a chance to see her in all her glory.

"That's definitely better," I said, as she crawled on the bed and came toward me.

"I barely slept because I couldn't stop thinking about you. About this." She stroked my face. "I know you need time, but don't you feel it? Don't you feel this?" She took my hand and squeezed it so hard that it hurt.

"Yes, but I still don't know what to think, Em. I'm sorry." She kissed my hand and then brushed some hair away from my face.

"That's okay. You don't have to think for a while. I'll do all your thinking for you." That sounded like an amazing plan. My brain worked way too hard all the time and anything that gave me a break was much appreciated. The fact that I also got to see tits was a bonus.

Emma kissed me softly. So softly that I pressed up to get more of her, but she held me down with one hand.

"Slow. We don't have to race. We have all night. Fuck sleep." I wanted to correct her and say that we were going to fuck instead of sleep, but I couldn't form the words.

"Just go slow." I could do that. I didn't have to do everything at a frantic pace just because that's how my brain usually functioned.

I could try, at least.

"Slow," I said, and she tenderly kissed me again. I held myself back from lunging at her and let her ply my lips with hers, taking small sips instead of big gulps of kisses. Her mouth cradled mine and took care of me. I kissed her back, falling into the slowness and enjoying it. Making out was so underrated. Teenagers had it right. Making out was awesome, and at least we didn't have to do it in the back of a car and worry if our parents were going to catch us.

Emma suckled on my bottom lip and I felt a shift in the air. She rolled on top of me and the shock of all of that skin was like jumping into a lake that was on fire. All my nerves overloaded.

"You okay?" she asked, because I'd stopped focusing on kissing her because there was so much skin contact happening. Especially in certain, more sensitive, places.

"Yup. Just . . . wow. Being naked with you is fucking awesome." It sounded silly when I said it, and she laughed a little.

"It is, isn't it? We have a lot of time to make up for, don't we?" We did. I didn't want to think about the fact that we could have been doing this for years. We could have been like this for years now. A sick feeling of regret churned in my stomach and I wanted to ignore it so it wouldn't poison our moment.

"Yeah, we do. Please kiss me again." I ran my hands up and down her soft arms. She was always so warm, and it was nice because I was always cold. As if we were created to perfectly balance each other out. Maybe we had been.

"If you insist," she said, and her lips met mine again.

∼

WE KISSED for what might have been hours. It was glorious and sweet and perfect, even if I forgot to breathe a few times and Emma had to remind me, and our hair got caught or in our mouths. It was still perfect. I ran my hands up and down her back, counting each knob of her spine. I wanted to know every single corner and crevice and curve of her body better than my own.

Emma's hands kept creeping further up my thigh and I started to laugh. She immediately pulled away from the kiss.

"Something funny?" she asked.

"Just you trying to be stealthy. I can feel where your hand is going, you know." We both looked down to see her stroking the inside of my left thigh. She wiggled her fingers in a little wave.

"I should hope you know where I'm going. Do you want me to keep going there?" she asked.

"Yeah, you can keep going where you're going. I'm on board. I'm completely on board. I kind of wish I was touching you like this instead, but I guess I'll take one for the team." She snorted.

"Yeah, I'm sure this is awful for you. A real sacrifice."

"It's true. I'm a saint." I fluttered my eyelashes at her and she fluttered her fingers upward and then I wasn't joking with her anymore.

"Saint Callyn, patron of puppies and pizza." I wanted to tell her that I liked that assessment, but I couldn't make my words work. I was too busy focusing all my attention on her tricky fingers that were making a slow and torturous travel up to where I needed them to be. I wanted to speed things along, but she'd said we were going to take things slow. I could do slow. I could be patient.

"Sweet Callyn, who I'm going to fuck," she said in my ear, before lightly nipping the lobe. I had died. She was touching my ghost. There was no way I could still be alive after she said that.

"Breathe, Cal," she said, kissing my neck and then working her way down my body. My thighs were pushed apart and she crouched between them, her fabulous ass in the air and a wicked smile on her face. This was an Emma I had never seen and I had been too overwhelmed with everything last night to register that part of it. The way her eyes changed and her energy changed and she turned into this vicious sex goddess who wanted nothing more than to murder me with pleasure. Perhaps that was what she did want.

"You ready, Cal?" she asked. No, I wasn't, but I nodded

anyway and gave in to the sex goddess that my Emma had turned into. It was the only thing to do, really.

She *did* devour me. She used her mouth and fingers and everything at her disposal to ravish me until I couldn't take it anymore and I did beg. I did. I begged and cried and promised her anything to just let me fucking come. I told her she was killing me. I told her I was going to die if she didn't touch me in the exact right way that I could totally instruct her on if she would just DO IT.

"You know, this is really interesting," she said, sitting up and wiping her face with one hand. Her hair was everywhere and I realized we both should have put ours up before we started. Notes for next time. I was probably going to have to write this shit down: Things To Do Before Sex. Number one, put up hair.

"What's interesting, you horrible, terrible, awful person?" I was panting and gasping and my entire body had started twitching, as if my circuits were mad that I wasn't having an orgasm.

"Seeing you beg and plead. Under normal circumstances, I'd do anything you asked, but right now, I'm enjoying this a lot. More than I thought I would." Her voice was calm, and she had the most satisfied grin on her face that I'd ever seen. I wanted to bite her and then make her feel this way so she would know how much it sucked.

"You're a monster," I said, and she shrugged one shoulder and just kept smiling.

"You have no idea." I swallowed a scream.

"Will you just let me fucking come already? I'm afraid something bad is going to happen to my body if I don't." Okay, so that was a lie, but not completely. My body had never felt like this and I wasn't sure it was okay to keep me in this heightened state without release for a long period of time.

"I guess I can let you come. But I'm going to make it happen again and again and again. I've been counting the days I could have given you orgasms and I have a number and I'm determined to get to that number." It was clear, she was definitely going to kill me.

"What's the number?" She leaned down and blew on my clit. My entire body jumped. I almost came from her *breathing* on me. I was that close.

"I don't think you're ready to hear it. But I'm keeping track. There's a spreadsheet." I was about to make a joke about spreadsheets, but then she plunged her fingers into me at the same time as she sucked my clit into her mouth and I came so hard that I screamed so loud, I hoped the neighbors didn't call the police. My body gave up everything but feeling complete and total pleasure so all-consuming that I didn't know if it would ever end. I rolled over the crest and started to come down, but it was still going, just softer, which was also good. The hardness had faded and now I was wrapped in a warm blanket of warmth and light and desire. Like sunshine. Slowly, the climax finally faded and I was left with tingling skin and a feeling as if everything was right and good in the world and nothing could ever be bad again.

"How was that?" Emma asked, and I tilted my head to look at her. She had rested her chin on one of my knees.

"I don't know if I can really talk about it yet," I said. My body was still trembling and glowing and sensitive. I loved this part almost as much as the orgasm itself. The aftermath.

"I'm judging by the screaming and the moaning and everything else that it was good for you?" She had been so confident moments before, but now she was asking me if my orgasm was good.

"Yes. It was good. It was beyond good. You couldn't tell?" Breathing was still a little bit of a struggle.

"I mean, I hoped there wasn't any exaggeration." I sat up.

"Excuse me? You think I could fake that shit? I'm not Meryl Streep." Emma gave me a weird look.

"Meryl Streep fakes orgasms?" she asked, and for some reason that made me burst out laughing.

"I don't think so, but I bet she could," I said, and she flopped on the bed next to me. "Oh are you done now? One orgasm and you're tapped out?"

She turned her head to the side and glared at me.

"Demanding little brat," she said.

"I'm your demanding little brat." Emma was interrupted from replying by a sad little yip from outside the door.

"Uh oh. The puppy has spoken." I got up and went to the door and opened it.

"Hello," I said to Vegas, who was wiggling with excitement that I'd listened to him. He'd even brought one of his favorite toys.

"Hi, sweet boy. Have you been waiting for us?" I wanted to pick him up, but I didn't really want to do that naked. I pulled Emma's robe off the back of the door and put it on.

"You're being a little clit-blocker," I said in an affectionate tone, as he licked my face. "Come see your other mama," I said, and Emma slid under the covers before I plopped the puppy in her lap.

"Hello, hello, yes, I know. You're a good boy." I loved the high little voice she used with Vegas. It was just so sweet and cute and it made me want to cry for some reason. Seeing them together gave me too many emotions. I usually had too many emotions, like I'd been born with an excess and I'd been trying to regulate myself since birth, but this, these moments when I saw her kissing his head, made everything in me overload.

"Do you want some tea?" I asked, so I could run away and wipe my eyes in private where she wouldn't see.

"Yeah, sure. Mid-coitus tea would be lovely." I went to the kitchen to boil some water in the electric kettle and found some tea that was supposed to support sexy feelings. I'd bought it as a joke and now I was happy that I had. I added some lemon and honey to the tea and got myself under control and made sure I didn't look like I'd been getting emotional before I went back to find Emma petting a sleeping puppy.

"Oh no. Now we can never move or have sex again," I said in a whisper, as I handed her the mug of tea.

"Nah, he's fine." I carefully got into bed with my tea. Vegas woke up a little bit, but then his eyes closed again when Emma started stroking the perfect part of his head that he loved.

"Thanks," she said, sipping. "This is nice, what is it?"

"Remember that sex tea I bought in that shop? This is it." Her eyes went wide.

"Oh, dear. Do you think we need it?"

"I mean, it couldn't hurt. We're already amazing at sex, so this is just a cherry on top. And it's probably just hot leaf juice that does nothing, but who cares? It's tea and it tastes good." She nodded and we lapsed into silence as Vegas snored.

"This is kind of perfect," she said.

"You haven't come yet." She almost choked on her tea.

"Doesn't matter. I don't have to come for sex to be amazing. Just being with you makes it perfect." I still had my robe on and she was under the covers, which was probably practical seeing as how we had hot beverages, but wasn't great because I couldn't see her body.

I petted Vegas and we drank our tea.

"What are you thinking about?" I asked. I wasn't sure if I

wanted to know, but I needed something to fill the silence. I hated silence.

"Just this. How I fantasized about us being together in bed, but I also thought about stuff like this. Just being naked with you. This intimacy." She looked over at me and smiled. "I like it and I'm scared it's going to go away."

Oh no, here we go again.

"Let's not talk about that right now. Let's finish our tea and evict the puppy and I want to make you come harder than you did for me. At least twice." Emma gulped down her tea and I laughed. I got up and moved the puppy, taking him out into the living room and setting him in his bed and then staying until he fell asleep again.

When I got back she was waiting for me, perched on her side like a seductress.

"I tried like three other positions before I landed on this one," she said, as my eyes went wide.

"You probably shouldn't have told me that. I'm the one who has to try too hard to be sexy. You just . . . are." I gestured to her.

"That's ridiculous. You're so sexy, Callyn. You don't even know." I rolled my eyes.

"I'm one of those girls who's pretty but isn't aware of it?" I walked toward her and leaned my arms on the edge of the bed.

"No, because that's insulting. What I mean is, that just do what your instincts tell you. It's all hot, I promise. I've seen a new side of you that I never thought I would. I like it. A lot." I could say the same about her.

"I like seeing new sides of you. Where have you been hiding Sexy Emma all this time?" She moved over so I could climb (hopefully sexily) on the bed next to her.

"She's been waiting for you to be ready," she said, stroking the side of my face. "I've been waiting for you for a long time." Well, that made me feel like shit. I didn't want to feel like shit, so I kissed her to distract myself.

I hadn't been waiting for her, I didn't think, but here I was, with her. I'd gotten her without even trying or wanting her. How the hell had I gotten so lucky? That was a sobering thought.

I kissed Emma hard and deep, and she let me. I kissed her frantically, unreservedly. I gave her everything I could possibly give, almost as an apology. I was sorry for not seeing her for all those years. For not seeing how she felt about me. For being so fucking oblivious. For maybe not knowing my own feelings, which were still unclear. I kissed her and then I pinched her nipples and started sucking on her neck and then made my way down her glorious body, tasting every inch before I moved on to the main event. She was so pretty here, so perfect. I didn't want to compare myself to her, but her downstairs was definitely superior to mine.

Instead of taking too much time to stare at her, I decided tasting was a much better idea. I waited for a moment to make eye contact with her so she could tell me if she wanted this or not. Even though we'd done this before, I didn't want to make any assumptions.

"You ready?" I asked. She widened her legs and nodded.

"Fuck, yes."

I took my time and teased her like she had for me. I could feel the contractions starting to come, could feel her legs trembling around my ears, but I didn't let her have it. I pulled back and kissed her thighs and then started the whole thing over. I discovered that even more than pressure, what drove her wild were little tongue flicks on either side of her clit along with deep strokes of my finger inside.

"Please, Callyn, please. I need it, I have to, *please*." She was right, begging rocked. I wanted to draw it out, but I also wanted to give her an orgasm so I could get her to the second in quick succession, so I fluttered my tongue on her clit and stroked her inside at the same time and kept going until I felt the contractions with my hand and my tongue and by her noises and movements. I wanted to raise my head and see her face, but I also wanted to keep this going, so I sacrificed my look and kept my tongue doing what she needed it to do.

This time she was screaming and I definitely heard my name. That almost made me come again. Holy shit was it great to hear someone say your name in the throes of a fantastic orgasm. Top notch moment.

When she quieted at last, I risked raising my head only to find her with a completely blissed-out smile on her face and a mist of sweat on her chest that made her glisten like some magical creature.

She stroked my sweaty hair and sighed.

"You're really good at that, Cal. I wanted to tell you that you were doing it perfectly, but I didn't have the power of speech. That was incredible. Thank you." I slid up her body and kissed her full on the mouth.

"You don't have to thank me, but hearing that I'm doing it right makes me feel like I can lift a fucking car or run a marathon or enroll in grad school." She giggled.

"Do you want to go to grad school?" she asked.

"I don't know, that was just a thing I said. Maybe? But I have no idea what I'd go for and I'm still in so much debt that it would be irresponsible to go without a goal and an intention." I hated the way those words sounded. I sounded like my disapproving parents, or my sister. She'd gone to grad school, but they'd completely supported that. Of course.

"You could, you know. You can do anything you want to. I want you to feel like you're supported. I know that your parents haven't been the best. We're alike in that at least." That was one of the things that had made us so close. Our parents weren't the best. They weren't the worst, but there was a long way from the worst to the best, with a lot of mediocre parenting in between.

"I don't know. I'm always just trying to keep my head above water. I never feel like I have time to breathe. Except when I'm with you." I kissed her cheek because it seemed like the right thing to do.

"That's how I feel about you. Like everything is spinning and with you I can stand still." I rested my head on her chest, right on top of her beating heart. It was racing, as was mine.

"I love you, Callyn. I know I'm probably not supposed to say that with all that you're thinking about, but I needed to say it. I love you, so much." I felt her lips on the top of my head and I wanted to cry again.

I did love her. I did. I just didn't know how much or in what way. Instead of running on that hamster wheel of thoughts again, I raised my head and kissed her.

"Fuck me again, please."

~

MUCH MUCH LATER, I woke up completely naked in Emma's bed. Fortunately, she was right next to me, so I was able to remember why I was naked and why I was in her bed. Right. The sex. We'd had the sex again. Twice in twenty-four hours. That was a record for me. I'd never had a sexual relationship like this before. All other encounters seemed like pale practice for what I did with Emma. What we had was on a whole other level of sex.

I needed to think about what was beyond the sex. Sure, that was fun and great and lovely and wonderful, but was it just sex? Clearly I had sexual feelings for her. That had been made clear by this second time and the fact that I wanted to wake her up and fuck her again and again until we both passed out from too much sex.

Okay, so I had that one figured out. I wanted to have sex with her. All the time, any time that I could. Forever.

I looked at her face in the glow of the still-lit salt lamps. The candles had burned themselves out long ago. It was that amorphous time between night and day, that gray in-between where everything seemed strange and unsure.

I watched Emma sleep, wondering what she was dreaming about. Was she dreaming about me? I hoped she was. I hoped she was thinking about what we'd done tonight and the night before and how she was finally getting what she wanted with me. Not all of it, though. I knew what she wanted. She wanted everything.

Was I ready to give her everything? I heard whining and went to the door to let Vegas in. I picked him up and put him on the bed, hoping he wouldn't wake Emma. He looked at her and seemed to realize that he should be quiet, so he put his head on his paws between us and I curled myself around him and stared at them both.

Here was my world. These two. In the past few months, everything had changed for me. I was living with my best friend, we were married on paper, we'd gotten a puppy, I'd gotten a new job, and now . . .

Now?

I let myself, just for a moment, picture a future with Emma. Instead of thinking of a wedding with someone else, with another person where Emma would stand next to me as my maid of honor, I thought about a wedding with her standing beside me. As my wife.

I thought about Christmas together, about buying a house together, doing life together. With Vegas and then maybe with kids. I still wasn't sure if I wanted them, but I went ahead and thought about it. Watching Emma teach them to ride bikes and swim in a pool. Wrapping presents from Santa and hoping they wouldn't wake up and catch us. Instead of stopping myself from seeing it, I let myself see it all in excruciating detail. I thought about waking up next to her ten years down the road, twenty, thirty, more. What would she look like as she aged? Of course, she would always be the most beautiful person I'd ever seen. That would never change.

What would that life be like? I had never expected it, never planned it, but here it was, in front of me for the taking. I could have all of those things if I just let myself have them.

It would be good. It would be wonderful. It would be more than I ever expected or could have imagined for myself. It would be more than I deserved, that was for sure.

I was scared too. Scared shitless. What if we tried this thing and it didn't work? I could understand why Emma had hesitated for so long. Because what was done couldn't be undone. If we didn't work out together, our friendship would be over. I didn't think I could be friends with someone I was once in love with. Breaking up with her would break me. I would never recover from that. It could all go wrong, it could all go bad.

But what if it went right? said a little voice in my head. What if we worked out? What if we looked back at this time and laughed about how foolish we were for so many years? What if we spent the rest of our lives together and lived happily ever after? Did such fairytales exist? Could they exist for us?

I didn't know the answer, but I did know one thing with clarity as I watched Emma and Vegas sleep: I wanted to give it a shot. I wanted to try. I wanted to see where this would go. The regret of "what if?" would kill me more than trying and then not having things work out. Regret would be worse than failure.

I also thought about other things as the light changed in the room and my eyes got heavier as exhaustion tried to take me under to sleep.

Maybe I could go to grad school. Maybe I could figure out what I really wanted to do with my life, with my time. I'd always just kind of bumbled around, but my parents had always been there, telling me what I could do and what I couldn't do and basically stomping on any kind of ambition I ever had. They gave all their support and attention to Dani, and it was like they didn't have enough left over for me. I still loved them, of course, but they hadn't been the parents I had needed them to be and I was going to be seeing the consequences of that for years to come, probably for my whole life. I should probably get myself into a therapist's office again to work some more of this shit out.

I'd always shied away from discussing my parents in therapy and that might have been a mistake. I was so tired of being scared and hesitant about things. It wasn't like me at all. I always wanted to do everything, right now. I would make a decision and then want to go full-throttle. Strange how I was hesitating with this whole Emma situation. This was one of the only times I hadn't just closed my eyes and jumped off the cliff.

I rested my head on the pillow that still smelled faintly of sweat and sex and closed my eyes finally. I didn't know what was going to happen when I woke up.

Chapter Thirteen

"Nope, not doing it," I said, when Emma's alarm rang a few hours later. I could do one night without sleep, but not two. It just wasn't going to happen. This was my second-to-last day and I was calling out sick. I'd have to go in the next day to clean out my desk and get my shit from the kitchen, so I was going to spend today sleeping.

"How did Vegas get in here?" A sleepy voice next to me asked. I turned my head to find a rumpled Emma blinking at me. Vegas was still here and he yawned and stretched before bounding all over the bed and licking both of our faces.

"I taught him how to open doors," I said, through a yawn. I felt like complete and utter shit. I did not want to be awake right now, but I'd needed that time last night to work through my shit and think about my future and what I wanted it to look like.

"Did you get up and let him in? We really shouldn't let him sleep in our bed," she said, but she was smiling as she scratched his ears.

"You know that you're going to lose that battle, Em." The blankets slid down and revealed her incredible boobs and I had to catch my breath. If I decided I wanted to be with her, I'd get to see her boobs. All the time. Every day.

"You're staring," she said, putting her finger under my chin and raising my chin.

"I can't help it. I've never seen your boobs this early in the morning." I'd never gotten to see Emma naked this early in the morning. I closed my eyes and took a deep breath.

"Okay, let's do it," I said, opening them.

"Do what?" Emma said, looking up from playing with Vegas.

"Let's be together." She seemed confused for a second.

"Do you love me?"

"I think so," I said, and instead of being overjoyed, she frowned.

"That's not good enough. I only want to be with you if you know you want to be with me, beyond a doubt. I won't accept anything less." I opened my mouth to argue with her, but then I shut it with a snap. She was right. I couldn't do this halfway. When the hell had I done anything halfway? Now wasn't the time to start, and definitely not when it came to love.

"Okay. I'll let you know when I know for sure. But until then, can we keep doing this?" She turned on her side and smiled.

"Can you be more specific?"

"This," I said, kissing her. "This." I squeezed one of her boobs and she yelped. "This." I stroked her between her legs and she made another noise altogether. "All of this." I stroked her again and she pushed into my hand. I was definitely awake now. Funny how sex could do that.

"I need to go to class," she said, but she wasn't stopping me at all.

"I mean, I haven't slept in two days and I'm definitely calling out of work. Speaking of that," I grabbed my phone, which had been charging on the nightstand and sent out a text to anyone who needed to know at my job that I wouldn't be in. I was sure Maggie would be upset that she couldn't soak up more of my wisdom, but that enthusiasm was going to get sucked out of her in four to six months, guaranteed. Poor thing. So young, so un-jaded.

I kept up my work on Emma with my other hand and she writhed and whined until I was done with the text and could really go for it. I had to push Vegas off the bed because it was weird having a puppy watching me finger fuck Emma. He cocked his head sideways and I wanted to tell him to look away. I ducked under the covers and started going down on her with my mouth. It got pretty hot under there pretty fast, but it didn't matter. I was going to make her come hard. She wasn't the only one who owed someone else orgasms.

This time I didn't try and draw it out. I went right for the kill, making sure I gave her entire clit and labia and entrance all of my attention while playing with my fingers, dipping them in and out in a teasing way before pushing inside and stroking the spot I knew would make her come, and come hard.

She did, shattering apart with a shout and I didn't wait for things to calm down before I stuck my head out and gulped on fresh air.

"Remind me not to do that again. I couldn't breathe. Totally worth it, though." I grabbed some tissues and wiped my mouth. We were going to have to keep extra face wipes around for moments like these.

"You didn't have to not breathe. You could have poked your head out." Her skin had a soft glow and her smile was radiant. Fuck, she was beautiful. It was such a relief to let myself have those thoughts. I think I'd ben subconsciously stopping them for years, and now the floodgates were open.

"Meh, breathing is secondary to getting you off." She sighed happily and stretched her arms over her head.

"Yeah, I could definitely get used to this."

I loved the look on her face. I wanted to give her that look every single day. She sighed and then dove at me.

"What the hell, Em?"

"Your turn," she said, and then I was on my back and she was crawling between my legs and I was getting pleasured so quick and so hard that I came in about thirty seconds.

"Oops. I meant for that to last longer," she said.

"No worries. We can always try again later. Practice makes orgasms." She laughed as my phone buzzed with a text from my supervisor. I could feel her irritation, but what could she do? Not a whole lot, I was done tomorrow. I'd get to have a whole weekend with Emma and then I'd be starting my new job on Monday. It was going to be great.

"Stay home with me," I said, throwing myself on her dramatically. "Stay home with me and Vegas." She bit her lip and looked at her phone.

"I don't know, I have a lot of work to do and I don't want to miss class." I could feel her caving, so I looked up and did my best attempt at a pout.

"Please?" I said. She huffed out a breath and scrolled through her phone.

"I just . . . I shouldn't."

"But you should," I said, taking her phone away and holding it out of her reach.

"Hey!"

"Phone away. No class. Only home." I gave the phone back and she glared at me.

"You're a bad influence."

"You're just figuring this out now?" I said. "I haven't been doing a very good job then."

She laughed and shook her head.

"You're ridiculous, and I love you." She hadn't been so free in saying it, but I guess she figured we'd crossed that bridge.

"I think I love you back," I said, and then cringed. "That sounded better in my head, sorry."

"No, it's okay. Just say it when you mean it. When you really mean it." She stroked my hair and I leaned into her hand. Yeah, I could really get used to this.

∽

FIGURING we should probably leave the apartment, we decided to go out for brunch, but we couldn't bring Vegas, so we left him in the bathroom with plenty of toys and food and water.

"We'll be back soon," I said to the saddest puppy ever. He knew something was going on. He was so smart.

"I feel horrible," I said to Emma, as we left the apartment.

"He'll be fine. He'll probably be sleeping in like five minutes and won't even remember that we left. And when we get back, he'll be so overjoyed that it won't even matter." She did have a point, but I still felt bad. My bad feeling was wiped away by the shock of Emma taking my hand.

"Oh," I said, as I twisted my fingers with hers, as if I'd done this every day for years. "This is new."

"It is. Do you like it?" I looked down at our hands. I couldn't tell whose fingers were mine for a second.

"I'll let you know," I said and swung our hands together like we were little kids.

Emma squeezed my hand and I squeezed hers back.

∽

WE CHOSE A FANCIER BRUNCH SPOT, but one that we didn't feel completely out of place in. We both got lobster benedicts along with fresh-squeezed juice and coffee.

"I'm still recovering from my caffeine overload, so I'm going to be good," I said. I had the feeling I was going to crash later and need a nap if we were going to spend a third night staying up late and fucking.

"To us," Emma said, holding up her juice glass.

"To us," I said, tapping my glass against hers. I couldn't resist dessert, so we ordered a piece of triple-chocolate cake to share, and I had to fight her to get bites with more frosting on them.

"I need it," I said by way of reasoning.

"You need more frosting?" she asked, dubious.

"Yes, I need it. For my . . . skin. It's good for the skin." Emma snorted.

"You are completely pulling that out of your ass, but I'll allow it."

"Thanks, wife," I said, and she started a little at the word. We hadn't talked about that particular facet of our relationship.

"We are married, aren't we?" she said, poking at a few crumbs left on the plate.

"Yeah, we are. We got drunk and that one night changed everything." It had been the catalyst to where we were today.

"It did." She wouldn't look me in the eyes.

"Do you think, maybe, that your subconscious pushed you toward it because you were in love with me?" It was something I hadn't really thought of until now, but maybe I should have.

"No, definitely not," she said too quickly. "You can have the last bite." Her smile was tight and brief. I knew that smile. It was her fake smile. Her "I'm fine" smile.

"Definitely not," I echoed, and she looked up at me.

"I didn't plan to get drunk and married in Vegas. Why would I do that?" Things had gone from lighthearted to intense and this wasn't what I wanted for today.

"We don't have to talk about it," I said. "Let's just forget about it." I ate the last bite of cake and our waiter brought the check. Emma snatched it before I could even try and reach for it.

"I've got this," she said, sliding her card into the little slot and setting it upright on the table.

Things between us were weird and she didn't take my hand when we left the restaurant, so I did it for her.

"Hey, I wasn't accusing you of anything. I was just asking a question. That's it." I made her stop walking and face me.

"I know. I just . . . none of this is how I saw it going in my head." That made me curious.

"How did you see it going?" She looked down and tried to hide a smile while her cheeks turned pink with a blush.

"Do you really want to know?"

"Hell yes I want to know." She started walking again, dragging me along with her into the park.

"Okay, well, it's kind of silly. So, I imagined you looking at me one day and realizing you had been madly in love with me our whole lives." Her grip on my hand was tight, but I let it happen. I wanted to hear this story and didn't want to distract her from telling it in any way.

"This is all just a fantasy. I didn't really think it would happen that way," she said quickly.

"It's okay, I'm not going to mock you or think it's ridiculous. Just tell me." I wanted desperately to know what her vision of the future might have been if I hadn't screwed it up by being so oblivious.

"Well, after you made a grand declaration of love, we would have tried to date like regular people, but it wouldn't have worked because we knew we were right for each other. I was going to surprise you with a proposal, but you would have also been trying to surprise me, and so we would have accidentally planned to propose on the same day. Of course, all our friends would have known and would have ensured that it went that way. There would be video and lots of pictures and tears involved. We both would have said yes, and then set a wedding date for not long after, because we couldn't wait. You would have moved in with me in the meantime and we'd be so happy that all our friends would be completely and totally disgusted and sickened by us. And then we'd get married, maybe on a beach, or in park, or on a mountain. I'd pictured it a dozen different ways." We stopped walking as we reached an empty bench and we both sat down. People buzzed and talked and walked and ran and carried on around us, but I was completely and totally focused on Emma and the future she was painting.

"The wedding wasn't the important part. It was that you were the one I was marrying. Everything else about it was just unimportant." We locked eyes and I leaned forward and kissed her. This was the first time I'd done that outside our respective bedrooms. It was different. Not that anyone was going to look twice at us, but I felt like people knew. That they could see our history written on both of us.

Emma hesitated for only a moment before she kissed me back. She took the hand that wasn't holding mine and pulled my face closer. Things started getting hot and heavy and I didn't think we should start ripping each other's clothes off in public, so I pulled back and opened my eyes.

"What was that for?" she asked. I wanted to look around and see if anyone was paying attention to us, but I didn't look away from Emma's eyes.

"Just because," I said. "Tell me more about how you saw our future." I loved hearing about it.

"After the wedding we would have gone someplace with

really good food where we could just eat and stay somewhere beautiful and have a lot of sex and maybe take some walks when we decided we needed to put clothes on. And there would be fireworks. I wanted there to be fireworks. After that? Being happy. Forever." She shook her head at herself.

"It sounds like something a little girl who wanted to be a princess would think up. Not a grown adult."

"No," I said, squeezing her hand. "It sounds wonderful. It sounds perfect."

Her voice quavered a little.

"Does it?" I nodded and had to choke down nameless emotions. Emma sighed.

"So, there you go. That's how I saw it. How did you see your life going?" I wasn't sure, honestly. When I was younger, I thought I would have a husband and then babies and do all of that, but then I realized I was a raging lesbian and that idea went out the window. So then I thought I might have a wife, and maybe not, and I might have kids, and maybe not. I didn't know where I wanted to live. I was never sure about anything. It was all too far in the future, too big, too adult. Too many enormous life decisions to be made that I wasn't ready for, even in the abstract.

"I don't know," I said. "I've changed my mind so many times that nothing ever stuck. I knew you'd be there, though. You'd always be there, no matter what."

She leaned over and kissed me.

"That's all I need to hear," she said. "Having you in my life is the most important thing." I agreed on that at least.

WE WALKED around the park and I made her go on the merry-go-round and then we walked down the street, stopping in any shops we fancied and talking and just enjoying being with one another. We kept holding hands the whole time and that was something to adjust to, but it was exciting. I liked having her fingers linked with mine for long periods of time.

"We should get home to the puppy," I said. He was probably really missing us and needed to go outside. If this hadn't been so last-minute, we might have been able to call Reece to watch him. She was coming over this weekend since the Bachelorette Babes had brunch on Saturday. I was really looking forward to it in some ways, but in others I was not ready to see my friends because they would immediately know what had happened with Emma. That wasn't even touching the fact that they had known she was in love with me and no one had hinted or said anything. I mean, I guess that was good since it protected Emma, but they might have dropped a few hints, at least. Something to help me get my head out of my ass sooner.

Emma and I went home and she decided it was time for lunch. I was definitely going to be taking a nap later as well.

"Is a kale salad with chicken, strawberries, and walnuts okay? I can make up some quick dressing for it too. And I'm in the mood to bake. You want dessert?"

I looked up from patting Vegas's belly.

"What kind of a question are you asking me, I can't understand you. Are you even speaking English right now?" I said, and she rolled her eyes.

"Okay, I get it. Also, it's a lot harder to surprise you with desserts now that we live together. So I'm declaring the kitchen a Callyn-free zone. You can't come in or watch what I'm doing." I walked toward the kitchen and she put her hands out.

"Stop," she said.

"In the name of love?" It was something I'd seen on a t-shirt once. "You can't stop me, Emma. I'm a force of nature." I made a swooshing sound like wind.

"Come on, stop. I want to play our game again." I stopped. This was clearly important to her.

"Okay, fine." I turned around. "But I'm probably going to smell what it is. My nose is very powerful." I heard her scoff.

"I don't think you'll guess this." That sounded like a challenge.

"I'll just be over here with my book." I wanted to read a book that wouldn't distract me too much from what Emma was doing, so I picked up the one about money. I'd probably have to read it multiple times to get the information to sink in, but that was okay. I could always renew it.

It was difficult to focus on the book and on Vegas, who was in play mode. He kept bringing me toys and I'd throw them, he'd scramble after them, and then we'd do it all over again. After the nap later, we needed to take him on a good long walk so he'd sleep tonight. Maybe go to the park that was close by.

The money book actually turned out to be hilarious and kind of mean, so I started paying attention and my brain clicked on so I shut out everything but the words on the page.

"Lunch is ready," a voice said right near my ear. I jumped up and dropped the book.

"What the fuck?" I looked to find an amused Emma.

"I was calling your name for a while, but you were completely lost," she said. That had happened before, too many times to count. Whenever I fell into my focus mode, you could scream my name a million times and I would not hear you.

"Sorry," I said, picking up the book from the floor before Vegas started chewing on it. I couldn't imagine the shame of taking a dog-chewed book back to them and then having to offer to buy a new copy.

"Good book?" she asked.

"Actually, yes. You should read it when I'm done."

"I should finish my Blind Date with a Book first. You know my rule, I don't read another book until I've finished all the books that I'm supposed to read." I stared at her for a second.

"What is that like?" I couldn't imagine.

"It's nice, you could try it." She leaned on the back of the couch and there was a soft smile on her face like she wanted to kiss me but wasn't sure if she should.

I was about to tell her that she could kiss me when she shook herself and glanced back into the kitchen.

"Lunch?" she said. Right, food. I was completely starving. I'd gotten so caught up in reading I'd forgotten about it.

"Yeah, lunch." I wanted to kiss her. I wanted her to kiss me. I wanted to spend a lot of the day kissing, but it seemed only fair that I should sort my shit out before we went down that road again.

We sat down together and had our salads.

"Where's the dessert?" I asked. Emma shrugged.

"I don't know, where could it be?" I gave her a puzzled look.

"Did you make it already?"

"Yup." Hmm. That meant that it was probably in the fridge. That narrowed my options down. Some sort of pudding? Mousse? That seemed too obvious.

"I'll figure it out, you just wait," I said.

"I'm not hearing any guesses, so you're not doing well so far," she said, and I wanted to poke her with my fork.

"Chocolate pudding?"

"No."

"Key lime pie?"

"No."

"Chocolate lime pudding pie?" That one made her laugh.

"No, but that's a good idea. I might have to try that one. I love chocolate and lime together." That did sound good. I should make more dessert suggestions. We could come up with the next big thing, whatever that would be.

I kept guessing, but I wasn't getting anywhere, and I wanted to know.

"Okay, I don't care. Just tell me," I said, when I put the dishes in the sink to rinse before putting them in the dishwasher. She'd already washed the pan she'd cooked the chicken in and cleaned up everything else. No clues here. She'd been too sneaky, and I'd been too oblivious, which was kind of how things went with us.

"First, you have to close your eyes." I narrowed them instead, instantly suspicious.

"This feels like a trap," I said.

"It's not, I promise. It's just dessert." I still wasn't sure, but I closed my eyes anyway. She opened the fridge and I heard it shut.

"Okay, now open them." I did and saw her holding a glass dish with something that definitely involved strawberries in it.

"I still don't know," I said, leaning down and looking through the clear pan and still at a loss.

"Strawberry pretzel salad," she said, putting the dish down on the counter.

"That's not dessert! Salad can't be dessert!" I pointed at her in accusation. "This *was* a trap!" Vegas ran into the kitchen and started barking, so I lowered my voice. I got excited sometimes and went a little overboard with my volume and I didn't want him to think we were upset.

"It's dessert, it is!" Emma said back, slapping my finger out of the way.

"I will have to taste it to reach my verdict," I said. "Slice me a piece of salad." Emma did and slid it onto a plate. It looked like strawberries on top, some sort of cream thing in the middle and then crushed pretzels on the bottom. Pretty clever.

"There was a girl at work who made this all the time and I stole her recipe. I've been wanting to make it for ages, but I didn't know what to do with the rest since I was living alone."

"You're not living alone anymore," I pointed out, scooping some of the "salad" up with my fork.

"Oh, shit this is good. This is really good." Everything she made was, but this was definitely going to become a favorite that she would have to make again.

"I thought you'd like it, and we had like a million strawberries kicking around in the freezer, so here we are." She made a plate for herself and we stood at the counter together eating. I kept catching her staring and it made me blush a few times. She still wanted to kiss me and I still wanted to let her.

I finished my plate and, instead of getting another slice, I took her not-finished plate from her and set it down.

"Hey, I wasn't done!"

"I have something else for you to do," I said, stroking her face to make my intentions clear.

"We shouldn't. Not until you figure things out," she said, her breath drenched in sweetness from the strawberries and cream.

"I can figure things out *and* kiss you, Em. Let's do both." I was a huge fan of doing a lot of things at once, especially if one of those things was kissing Emma.

"Just a little kiss," I pleaded. "Just a tiny one. The littlest kiss. So small. Microscopic. You won't even know it's a kiss." Emma laughed a little.

"You're really selling this kiss thing hard."

"Is it working?"

She exhaled and smiled.

"Yes," she said before planting her lips on mine. I was supposed to be doing that, but whatever. I melted into her, pressing our bodies together and backing her up until she was against the wall.

"We're not doing this again," Emma said in a rush as she broke the kiss for a moment.

"Right, yeah, this is just kissing." I nodded in agreement.

"Absolutely. Just kissing."

"Uh huh," I said, and then we were kissing again.

∽

A FEW HOURS LATER, we were in Emma's bed again and we were both completely naked and we'd fucked again. Oops?

"We kind of failed at that, didn't we?" she said, looking at me. Both of us were still covered in sweat from the sex and I really needed a shower.

"Failed at what?" I still had sex brain and wasn't thinking as quickly as I usually did.

"Just kissing."

"Oh, yeah. We blew past that pretty quick." Really quick. I don't remember who got naked first, but it happened and here we were.

"Any regrets?" she asked, turning toward me.

"Nope," I said. "Not even a little bit."

"Good. Same." She put her hand up and I wasn't sure what I was supposed to do, so I gave her a high five. She giggled and then reached for my hand again, twisting our fingers together.

"There," she said with satisfaction. "Now all is right with the world."

"Agreed."

Chapter Fourteen

I GOT through my last day at the awful job, and said goodbye to Linda, Jessika, Maggie, and the rest of the people that I actually liked. I didn't bother with the ones that I couldn't stand and was grateful to never see again. Time to cross that bridge and burn the shit out of it.

On Saturday, Reece came over to watch Vegas and said she'd start work on some basic obedience while we were gone. She also was going to take him to the park, so he was one spoiled boy.

Brunch was at a pub, which was cozy and delicious. The second Emma and I walked in (we were the last to show up), everyone stared at us.

"How are you doing?" Nova asked, in a weird voice. Lara's gaze was bouncing from me to Emma and back, Willa was grinning, and Sammi looked like she wanted to scream in excitement.

"Okay, you all can calm the fuck down," I said. "This is not a big deal."

"Yes it is!" Sammi yelled, grabbing me up in a hug.

Emma and I had decided to play things cool, but I guess the news was written all over us.

"Tell us everything," Willa said, as we sat down at a table together.

"You want to take this one?" I asked, looking at Emma, who was blushing and smiling and shaking her head at our friends.

"No, you've got this," she said. "The floor is yours." Of course it was.

"Okay, then I'm telling them what's going on." She gestured in a "go ahead" motion.

So I told them. I told them that we had kissed and had sex and that I was working on my shit and figuring it out. I didn't give them graphic details, but they still got the gist as we dined on eggs fried in tons of butter and fresh-baked biscuits and thick sausages.

"So that's the gist of it. I will not be taking questions or comments at this time." I looked over at Emma, who was grinning again.

"Okay, but we have, like, a million questions," Sammi said. Nova put a hand on her shoulder.

"I think we should save the questions for another time."

"You dumbasses better not fuck up my wedding," Lara said and that earned her a sharp look. "What? I don't have time to rearrange bridesmaids and deal with other shit. I'm at the end of my rope." She burst into tears and then the heat was off me and Emma, which was nice. We had a mini therapy session with Lara, who was breaking under the wedding pressure, and we managed to make her laugh and give her the support that she really needed. After we ate, we all headed to a farmer's market that also had live music and great food trucks. Not that we needed any more food, but I was dying for some fried Oreos at the very least.

Emma and I didn't hold hands on the walk over, but it felt like we should have.

"What is the protocol?" I asked her when we reached the market, and all pulled out our tote bags to fill them up with fresh produce.

"The protocol for what?" she asked, looking at some completely enormous heirloom tomatoes in various colors ranging from a sunshine yellow to a deep purple with green accents.

"The protocol for us being with our friends. We've held hands in public, why not now? It's not like they don't know." She glanced up from the tomatoes.

"I was giving you space to think. I keep trying to do that and you keep seducing me." I gasped dramatically.

"Excuse me? I think you're the one who's doing the seducing, Emma Christine."

"Are you serious right now?" Her voice was a little loud and people were staring, including our friends, who weren't even pretending to sort through the fresh herbs.

"Fine, I won't hold your hand or kiss you or act like I like you in any way, happy?" She picked up a tomato and for a second I thought she was going to throw it at me.

"You don't have to do that, but I thought you were the one who had to figure out her feelings." She grabbed a bag and put the tomato in it and started picking some others.

"I do! But I can figure out my feelings while making out with you and holding your hand in public." A woman behind me made a disgusted noise. Mind your business, Brenda.

Emma gave me a look and picked another tomato.

"There's a guy selling figs over there who I don't think heard you." I made a frustrated noise and almost smashed my face into a wooden box of peppers. That probably wouldn't be too pleasant for my eyes.

Instead I mumbled and grumped and was insufferable

for the rest of the time we were out with our friends. I just wanted to go home and cuddle our puppy.

"You're being a dick," Nova said. "Get your shit together." She gave me a hug and a glare, and Sammi pretty much said the same thing.

"Get your shit together before my wedding," Lara said.

"I don't have my shit together, so I can't really tell you to, but I wish you would figure things out so you could just be happy together," said Willa. Things had gone well with the bartender, and they were tentatively seeing each other. I was happy for her.

"Okay, I'll get my shit together, god," I said to all of them, before storming up the street with Emma.

"I know they're right, that's why I'm so mad," I said to her.

"It's okay, a lot has happened in a short period. You're allowed to take your time to figure things out. I had a lot of years to get where I am." That was true. I was frustrated that I was expected to just KNOW. To just go forth. Granted, that's what I usually did, but this was different. This was love. Love was the most important thing in the world, and this was a decision that would completely alter the entire course of the rest of my life. You didn't make those things lightly, and I couldn't be with her unless I was sure.

I didn't know how to *get* sure. What was it going to take?

∽

I WAS TRAINING with my new boss at the co-working space on Monday when I got a phone call. They said it was fine to have my phone on, but I didn't recognize the number, so I sent it right to voicemail, and went back to what I was doing. Five minutes later, another call.

"Are you sure you don't want to take that?" my new boss, Sofia, asked.

"They left a voice mail, hold on," I said. This better be an emergency and not some fucking phishing scam. I was going to rip someone a new asshole if it was. I didn't want to make a bad impression on my first day.

I started listening to the voicemail and nearly dropped the phone.

"Oh shit, oh shit, oh fuck," I said, not even trying not to swear. The voice on the other end of the phone said that there had been an accident and they were calling to speak to Emma Vitali's wife, and to get to the hospital. *I* was Emma Vitali's wife.

"What's wrong?" Sofia said as I stared at them, completely stunned.

"My . . . my . . .my wife has been in an accident and is at the hospital." Sofia grabbed my hands and squeezed my fingers.

"I'm so sorry, which hospital?"

"Uh, MGH," I said. I think that was what the person on the other end of the phone had said.

"Okay, let's go. I'll call you a car and we can go together. You shouldn't be alone right now." I blinked at them, unable to process their words. They basically picked me up and shoved me outside and onto the street and then into the backseat of a car. The nurse from the hospital hadn't said how serious Emma's injuries were. Why hadn't she said how serious the injuries were?! What the fuck was wrong with Emma?

Sofia got me into the hospital and shoved me down the hall and found out where Emma was.

"Emma!" I screamed when I saw her lying in a hospital bed. Her eyes were closed and she looked so pale. She was in a little curtained-off area in the ER, but the other sections were empty. I threw myself onto the available space on the bed. Her hair was a mess and she was so very still.

"Oh my god, Emma, you have to wake up. You have to. You have to wake up so I can tell you that I love you." I knew now. This was the moment. When I'd been in that car and driving to the hospital, everything had fallen into place. It was so obvious, later I would be pissed at myself for ever doubting it. Right now, I was still flipping out and begging her to open her eyes so I could see if they were shading toward blue or green today.

"Ow," she said with a groan, as her eyes opened. Blue. They were so blue.

"Fuck, you're not dead," I said, instantly bursting into tears again. "You can never die, I won't let you." I wanted to hold her so tight and never let her go, but that probably wouldn't be pleasant for her right now. Later, after she healed from whatever had happened. She would heal. I would do whatever it took to help her.

"Okay," she said in a rough voice with a smile. "When did you get here?"

"Just now. What happened, Em?" She sighed and cringed, as if it hurt.

"Ugh. There was a bunch of wind and one of those huge construction signs flew into the windshield of the car I was in and we ended up crashing. That's what I get for being lazy and not wanting to walk to campus. The driver is okay, I think, but it was really bad there for a little while. I was so scared and all I could think about was coming back to you. I love you so much, Callyn, all I wanted was to get to you."

I guess she hadn't heard my declaration of a few moments ago so it was time to make it again, this time so she could hear me. It was time for us.

I took a breath. "I love you, Emma. I do. I know now. I promise. This is it. You're it. You're everything to me, always have been." I wanted to stroke her hair and hold her, but I didn't know the extent of her injuries, so I didn't want to hurt her.

Her smile was the most beautiful thing I'd ever seen in my life. It made my heart want to burst in my chest. At least we were already in the hospital.

"You don't know how long I've waited to hear you say that." She lifted one arm and wiped away some tears from my face.

"Are you okay?" I asked, taking more stock of her. Her face was unblemished, but there was an IV in her arm. I tried not to think through all the terrible injuries she could possibly have suffered.

"Yeah, I'm fine. Sort of. Just a broken leg, probably, and maybe some other stuff. I have to go for tests, so I'm just waiting for them to take me. I was knocked out for a little bit there, so I probably have a concussion." I squeezed her hand and brought to my lips, kissing it. I was afraid to touch her anywhere else. I couldn't imagine causing her any more pain.

"But you're going to be okay?" I said, and she nodded, but winced.

"Ouch, why did I do that?" She tried to lift her hand to touch the back of her head, but then she winced again.

"Everything hurts, Cal."

"I'm going to take care of you," I said. I had no idea what that would entail, but if she needed a fucking kidney, I would grab a scalpel and cut it out of me for her right now.

"Did someone call you?" Emma asked, and I told her about Sofia, who was absent. I guess they'd stepped out to give us privacy.

"What a way to start a new job, huh?" I said, and she laughed then winced.

"Maybe a cracked rib or two," she said.

"Okay, you keep adding injuries and I'm getting

concerned. Let's call a nurse so I can get the full details on my busted wife." The word was so natural now, so easy. She agreed and I hit the call button. A very nice nurse in scrubs with llamas on them came in and gave me the litany of Emma's injuries and her possible injuries. It was nice that we were legally married because I might not have gotten that info otherwise. I also realized that as her wife, it was my duty to call her parents and tell them what had happened.

Another nurse arrived to take Emma down to get a bunch of scans and x-rays taken to ascertain the extent of what happened, so I said I would let her do that and call her parents.

"Are you going to tell them?" she asked.

"Do you want me to?" She thought about that for a second.

"Sure, fuck it. Tell them. Tell them we're in love and we eloped after you tell them the other stuff. I mean, can they be mad that we're married after you tell them I've been in an accident?" She had an excellent point. It would probably go right over their heads.

"Okay, will do," I said, and leaned down to give her a good luck kiss. "I love you."

"I love you, Callyn Jean," she said, her voice choked with emotion. "Always will."

∽

THE CONVO with Emma's parents was a little chaotic. They were so panicked about Emma being in the hospital that I sort of threw in the marriage thing, but I could tell that it didn't resonate, so they were going to find out when they got here, which would take a few hours. I said I was staying with her and they thanked me. They weren't bad people, they just had bad priorities for their only daughter.

Sofia also stayed with me and I thanked them over and over again until they told me to stop.

"I don't even know you and this is my first day, but you're doing all of this. Don't you have an office to run?" They waved that off.

"Look, work isn't everything. That's probably not what other bosses would say, but it's not. I used to work a job that sucked up all my time and energy and I gave and gave and gave and I didn't pay attention to my husband and then he had a massive heart attack when he was thirty-five. I lost him and I lost that time because I put work first. Yes, your job is important, but the things outside of work are more important." I had never met a boss who talked like that. I think I was going to like this job.

"I'm here to support you, in whatever way that is. Right now it's being here. Down the road it might be helping you gain new skills so you can be better at your job. It might be a million different things, but that's *my* job." They said it like that was no big deal. Wow.

"This is the weirdest first day of work I've ever had," I said, and we both laughed.

"It will only go up from here, I promise," they said, and I believed them.

~

EMMA HAD a fractured leg and two cracked ribs, a concussion, and some bruising, but no internal bleeding, so that was great. She was going to be fine after a short hospital stay, and then we were going to have some recovery time. She'd already emailed her professors and taken medical leave. I asked Sofia if I could have a few days off to take care of her and they didn't have to let me, but said that they would, and I gave them a hug, which probably wasn't appropriate, but I didn't care. They had been here for me today and I didn't know if I would have been able to get through it without their help.

They moved Emma into a room and I hung out with her and watched bad TV and brought her food when she wanted snacks. I also found out where the nurses got their coffee from and got myself a cup, as well as one for Emma.

Her parents showed up and her mom was a complete wreck, and her dad gave me a tight smile. We'd known each other for so long, but it was still a little awkward being around them. Especially now that I was married to their daughter and in love with her and they had no idea.

"Mom, I'm going to be okay. I have Callyn," Emma said, throwing me a look.

"Yeah, I'm going to take good care of her." I tried to ask Emma with my eyes if I should tell them about the marriage and the love, but I don't think she got the memo.

"Mom, dad, I have something to tell you," she said, reaching out to me.

"Oh, are we doing this now?" I asked, but I went to her.

"Yeah, we're doing this now. No better time." I took her hand and squeezed it. I looked at her parents and they were giving us confused looks.

"We're together. And we're married," Emma said.

"You're what?!" her mother screeched, and Emma's father put his hand on her shoulder.

"Cheryl, calm down. Let's not make a scene." They really didn't like scenes.

"You're married? When did you get married? Were you going to tell us? What is going on with you, Emma?" I looked at Emma and she just gave me a smile. I think she was on some pretty decent painkillers that had just kicked in.

"You want to take this one?" she asked, and closed her

eyes. "I'm suddenly very tired." With that, she fell asleep, and I had to deal with my new in-laws.

∼

IT TOOK a lot of talking and reiterating what had happened and the fact that, yes, I did love their daughter, and no, I hadn't always known it myself. They hadn't known Emma was in love with me, but they weren't surprised after the initial shock.

They actually took it better than I thought they would, and Emma eventually woke up.

"I have to go get Vegas soon," I said, looking at the clock. The day had flown by somehow. I didn't want to get the puppy and then have to go home and be in the apartment by myself, but that was what I was going to have to do. I didn't like it.

"Listen, just video chat me. That way it's like we're together, and then I can see Vegas." That was a perfect idea.

"What's Vegas?" Emma's mom asked.

"We got a dog," Emma said. "It's not a big deal." I could feel Cheryl wanting to say something else, but her husband hushed her and ushered her out of the room and into the hall to give us some privacy.

I agreed that I would video chat with Emma as soon as I got back, and kissed her until we were both completely breathless, and not just because Emma had a few cracked ribs.

"I'm going to miss you so much," I said, even though I'd be back here tomorrow as soon as I could drop Vegas off. Everything else was going to be on hold while I took care of Emma. Her parents were going to stick around in case she needed anything as well, so I would have to keep dealing with them. I guess since they were my in-laws now, I'd have to adjust to it.

Vegas was so happy to see me, and I felt horrible when he ran around the apartment like he was looking for Emma.

"She's not here, but she's in the phone, come here, sweetheart." I called Emma and she came up immediately.

"Hey," she said. Sounded like she'd had another round of painkillers.

"Look, it's mama," I said to Vegas, and he started licking the phone.

"Okay, okay!" I pulled it away from him and tried to get off the worst of the slobber.

"Sorry about that."

"It's okay," Emma said through a yawn. Something told me this was going to be a short conversation.

"Before you completely pass out, I want to remind you that I love you, and I love our life together and I love you and I love you." I couldn't stop saying it now.

"I love you and I love you and I love you," she mumbled, her eyes half-closed. Oh, she was cute when she was doped up. I was going to enjoy that a little too much.

"Goodnight, my love," I said. She yawned again and the phone fell to the bed and the chat ended.

∽

SHE WAS a little more chipper the next day, and had her cast on and her ribs wrapped when I got there. I had to help her to the bathroom, and she got mad at me for helping her and not calling for a nurse, but I said I was her wife and I had the privilege of helping her pee when she needed help. Someday, she could pay me back.

Emma was in the hospital for a whole week, and then her ribs had healed enough for her to get around with crutches and we went home. Vegas was beyond confused by the cast and kept trying to bite it, but he couldn't do much damage.

"I can't wait until I have just a brace on it. I want to take a normal shower." Every time she needed to bathe, we had to wrap up the cast in a bunch of bags and it was a whole production that always had me laughing and Emma frustrated. She was not a good invalid.

We ended up ordering a lot of food because I was too tired from taking care of her and the puppy to cook. Whatever, I was putting it all on my credit card. The pay at my new job would take care of it, when I eventually was able to work and get paid. I'd been in contact with Sofia and they had been so great about everything.

Reece was actually coming over tomorrow so I could get back to work. Our other friends were also taking shifts to make sure Emma could get to the bathroom and didn't have any emergencies. I was also one phone call away, and could come home if she needed me.

"This was not what I planned," Emma said, after one week of being home from the hospital and fumbling around with the crutches.

"I don't think most people plan to fracture their leg and crack their ribs, Em," I said, as she slowly toppled over on the couch.

"I know. But I still don't like it. Although, one good thing did come out of all this," she said, as I sat down next to her and started playing with her hair.

"What's that?" I asked.

"You finally figuring out that you loved me." Oh, that.

"I mean, it probably shouldn't have taken you getting in a car accident for me to get my shit together." She laughed.

"At least you got there," she said, looking over her shoulder at me.

"I did. You're my wife, my go home, my ride-or-die, my

everything, my forever, my one true love, my best friend." Our eyes locked and we had one of those moments that seemed to stop time.

"It was worth all the pain to hear you say that, Callyn. You're my best friend too." That was the most important because it was where we had started. No matter what else Emma was to me, she was always that.

"Oh, by the way, getting married was my idea," Emma said. "I was drunk, but I remember everything."

"What?!"

Epilogue

One month later, I walked down the aisle in a dusty rose bridesmaid dress at Lara's wedding, but I wasn't looking at anyone in the crowd. I had my eyes locked with one person. Emma, who had walked down (with a massive boot on her leg that the dress couldn't hide) just before me. I couldn't wait to walk down the aisle to her again, and be sober this time. We had a celebration planned in six months, and we decided that we wanted to renew our vows in Vegas every year for the rest of our lives. This time we were going to bring the dog.

Her parents had stopped flipping out about us being married, just in time for me to tell my parents about us being married. I got the mother of all lectures, but I didn't care. Somehow their words didn't sting like they usually did. I even got congratulated by my sister, which was a complete shock. We ended up chatting on the phone for over an hour, and I had some hope that maybe we could start a relationship.

Vegas was killing it at puppy school, and I was so proud of him and glad he was in our life, even if I had to get up and take him out at all hours.

My new job was amazing, and Emma was killing it at vet tech school. Financially we weren't in the best situation, but Emma wanted to get a part time job for a few hours a week to help, and I was flirting with the idea of going back to school after she'd graduated. Still wasn't sure what I was going to do, but I wanted to do it. I wanted to give myself a new challenge and see what I could really do with my brain and my talents if I was given a shot and not constantly told that I shouldn't or couldn't.

When I reached Emma, I used the hand that wasn't holding my bouquet to twist our fingers together in the folds of our dresses.

"I love you," I whispered.

"I love you," she whispered back, as Lara and Asa said their vows. Next time we got married, I was going to write my own vows and pour out my heart to her in front of everyone we cared about. I felt this strange need to prove to everyone that our marriage wasn't a mistake that we were just going along with because divorcing was too much work. I wanted our love to be legitimate. Emma said that was bullshit, and I loved her for it.

Lara and Asa kissed while everyone cheered and then we were walking back down the aisle, but Emma and I walked together, instead of single file. I hoped Lara wouldn't be mad, but I wanted to walk down the aisle with my wife. Again.

Like this book? Reviews are SO appreciated! They can be long or short, or even just a star rating. Thank you so much!

Want another Boston romance? Try Anyone but You!

Sign up for my newsletter for access to free books, sales, and up-to-date news on new releases!

Acknowledgments

Surprise! I wrote a book. I wrote a book during one of the most difficult times of my life. I wrote a happy-sweet thing even when there was a broken heart beating in my chest. I can't thank my friends and my mom enough for being there for me. A huge shoutout to my coworkers at my dayjob for being unfailingly supportive as well. Thanks go to Laura, for editing this thing and making sure I got it right, and for my Patreon subscribers who are amazing. Thanks to my author friends, especially Magan Vernon, for being incredible and sending me advice and gifs and picking me up when I was really, really down. Lastly, thank YOU for reading this! I hope it gave you a few moments of joy and an escape from the burning planet and the general awfulness of everything. That is my only goal, and if I have succeeded, then writing this book was worth it.

About the Author

Chelsea M. Cameron is a New York Times/USA Today Best Selling author from Maine who now lives and works in Boston. She's a red velvet cake enthusiast, obsessive tea drinker, vegetarian, former cheerleader and world's worst video gamer. When not writing, she enjoys watching infomercials, singing in the car, tweeting (this one time, she was tweeted by Neil Gaiman) and playing fetch with her cat, Sassenach. She has a degree in journalism from the University of Maine, Orono that she promptly abandoned to write about the people in her own head. More often than not, these people turn out to be just as weird as she is.

Connect with her on Twitter, Facebook, Instagram, Bookbub, Goodreads, and her Website.
If you liked this book, please take a few moments to **leave a review**. Authors really appreciate this and it helps new readers find books they might enjoy. Thank you!

Other books by Chelsea M. Cameron:

The Noctalis Chronicles

Fall and Rise Series

My Favorite Mistake Series

The Surrender Saga

Rules of Love Series

UnWritten

Behind Your Back Series

OTP Series

Brooks (The Benson Brothers)

The Violet Hill Series

Unveiled Attraction

Anyone but You

Didn't Stay in Vegas

Wicked Sweet

Christmas Inn Maine

Bring Her On

The Girl Next Door

Who We Could Be

Castleton Hearts Series

Didn't Stay in Vegas is a work of fiction. Names, characters, places and incidents are either the product of the author's imagination or are use fictitiously. Any resemblance to actual persons, living or dead, events, business establishments or locales is entirely coincidental.
No part of this book may be reproduced, scanned or distributed in any printed or electronic form without permission. All rights reserved.
Copyright © 2019 Chelsea M. Cameron
Editing by Laura Helseth
Cover by Chelsea M. Cameron

Printed in Great Britain
by Amazon